DATE DUE

The Library Store #47-0119

MELVIN BEEDERMAN SUPERHERO

BOOK 1: THE CURSE OF THE BOLOGNA SANDWICH

BOOK 2: THE REVENGE OF THE McNASTY BROTHERS

BOOK 3: THE GRATEFUL FRED

BOOK 4: TERROR IN TIGHTS

BOOK 5: THE FAKE CAPE CAPER

BOOK 6: ATTACK OF THE VALLEY GIRLS

BOOK 7: THE BROTHERHOOD OF THE
TRAVELING UNDERPANTS

www.melvinbeederman.com

MELVIN BEEDERMAN SUPERHERO #8

INVASION FROM PLANET DORK

GREG TRINE

ART BY

RHODE MONTIJO

HENRY HOLT AND COMPANY ★ NEW YORK

To my brother Danny
—G. T.

To my super friends
Bloated Ninja, King Keg,
and Monkey Boy
—R. M.

Henry Holt and Company, LLC
Publishers since 1866
175 Fifth Avenue, New York, New York 10010
www.HenryHoltKids.com

Henry Holt® is a registered trademark of Henry Holt and Company, LLC.
Text copyright © 2010 by Greg Trine
Illustrations copyright © 2010 by Rhode Montijo
All rights reserved. Distributed in Canada by H. B. Fenn and Company Ltd.

Library of Congress Cataloging-in-Publication Data
Trine, Greg.
Invasion from planet Dork / Greg Trine ; art by Rhode Montijo. — 1st ed.
p. cm. — (Melvin Beederman, superhero ; bk. 8)
Summary: As big trouble heads toward Los Angeles, California,
Melvin Beederman gathers his superhero friends to face
what comes—a trio of extraterrestrial kidnappers who
call themselves Monkey Wrench, Elbow, and Shoe.

ISBN 978-0-8050-8165-7 (hardcover)
1 3 5 7 9 10 8 6 4 2

ISBN 978-0-8050-8167-1 (paperback)
1 3 5 7 9 10 8 6 4 2

[1. Superheroes—Fiction. 2. Extraterrestrial beings—Fiction.
3. Kidnapping—Fiction. 4. Los Angeles (Calif.)—Fiction.
5. Humorous stories.] I. Montijo, Rhode, ill. II. Title.
PZ7.T7356Inv 2010 [Fic]—dc22 2009019488

First Edition—2010 / Hand-lettering by David Gatti
Printed in April 2010 in the United States of America by
R. R. Donnelley & Sons Company, Harrisonburg, Virginia

CONTENTS

1	Pretzel Problems	1
2	A Cry for Help	11
3	Superheroes on Patrol	18
4	Meanwhile . . .	26
5	Who Do We Kidnap?	32
6	Stinky Alien Feet	42
7	Follow That Smell!	48
8	Holy Disappearing-Spaceship!	54
9	Alien Rock and Roll	62
10	*Zap!*	69
11	Four Superheroes Are Better than Two	77
12	Hugo to the Rescue	85
13	Who's That Alien?	93
14	Alien Dog Pile	102
15	*Crash! Splat! Thud! Kabonk!*	109
16	Candace Makes Her Move	116
17	The Journey Home	131

PRETZEL PROBLEMS

Superhero Melvin Beederman had been enjoying a long shower while singing one of his favorite Grateful Fred songs, "Love Is a Nose but You Better Not Pick It." All was well in his world.

He toweled off, rubbed some Melvin Mousse into his hair to form a perfect M, flexed in front of the mirror, and went to see about breakfast.

Was there a pretzel in the house?

1

There was not. That's what you call an emergency.

"Holy this-is-an-emergency!"

Holy this-is-an-emergency, indeed! It sure was. Even Melvin's pet rat, Hugo, had something to say on the subject.

"Squeak," he said with a twitch of his whiskers. This either meant "Get me some pretzels and make it snappy," or "You were a little flat on 'Love Is a Nose but You Better Not Pick It.'" Melvin was never exactly sure what Hugo was saying. He just knew he wanted pretzels as much as his rat did. Maybe more.

Melvin and Hugo lived together in a tree house overlooking the city of Los Angeles, where Melvin saved the world on a daily basis, with the help of his trusty sidekick, Candace Brinkwater. But this morning, work would have to wait. He needed to stock up on snacks so that he and his pet could start the day off properly—eating pretzels, drinking root beer, and watching their favorite TV show, *The Adventures of Thunderman.*

"I'll be back in a flash," Melvin said to Hugo, as he launched himself out the window. "Up, up, and away!"

Crash!

He hit the ground hard. He got to his feet and tried again.

"Up, up, and away!"

Splat!

He hit the ground even harder.

Once more.

"Up, up, and away!"

Thud!

And again.

"Up, up, and away!"

Kabonk!

On the fifth try he was up and flying. This was how it went with Melvin Beederman. It always took him at least five tries to get up and flying. But no matter. He was up in the air now and on a mission, which is the same thing as being on a pretzel run, but mission sounds better, so we'll go with that.

As he streaked across the sky, Melvin looked down, and what did he see? Underwear—and lots of it. He couldn't turn off his x-ray vision, so he saw everyone's underwear whether he wanted to or not.

But underwear was the least of his problems. Something didn't feel right. Melvin could sense when trouble was brewing, and right now it was—or at least it was about to be. He didn't care if trouble was brewing or if it was just *thinking* about brewing. Trouble was trouble and it was his job to do something about it.

While Melvin was busy on his snack food errand . . . uh, mission . . . and feeling that something was not quite right, evil was lurking a few million miles away. A million miles may seem like a long distance, but not when you have a spaceship powered by Gamma Drive. And this was just what some evil aliens had. They'd stopped for gas and snacks at Alpha Centauri and were now headed to Earth to engage in sinister and devious deeds. They hadn't decided which it would be

yet and were playing Rock Paper Scissors
to figure it out.

"Ready? Go," said one
of the aliens named
Monkey Wrench.

His real name was Zzykrkv, but that was just way too hard to pronounce—especially in a children's book. Before deciding to invade Earth, he and his two companions had found an English dictionary on the Galaxy Wide Web and chosen new names so they could blend in. Monkey Wrench's companions were

named Elbow and Shoe, because Przzt and Cryykt were just too weird.

Monkey Wrench was the leader. Elbow was second in command and was referred to as Number Two, since he hadn't showered in a few Gamma Years. (He was an alien version of the McNasty Brothers, if you want to know the truth.) Shoe was third in command and the officer in charge of laundry and cooking.

"Anyone care for a Zig Newton?" Shoe asked. "Fresh out of the oven."

"Later. We have to decide if we're going to be sinister or devious," Monkey Wrench said.

"Rock Paper Scissors. Ready? Go."

They went. Rock won. "Sinister, it is."

The aliens were coming from their home planet, Dork. They were on a mission to kidnap a few Earthlings for science class, and they figured Los Angeles, California, was as good a place as any to start looking for the right specimens. This was bad news, of course—bad news for Melvin Beederman and his superhero assistant, Candace Brinkwater, because they were in charge of protecting the city.

A CRY FOR HELP

Melvin had felt strange all day. After returning from his pretzel run . . . uh, mission . . . he had eaten breakfast with his rat, Hugo, while watching an episode of *The Adventures of Thunderman.* Thunderman and his assistant, Thunder Thighs, always ended up on top. This inspired Melvin to get out there and save the world, even on rainy days!

But today he felt something was off.

Something was coming—something devious, something sinister, something that smelled bad.

Melvin could hardly keep his mind on his work, which, of course, was catching bad guys. He had been flying over the city all morning. Finally, he landed on one of the tall buildings downtown and reached for his pretzel phone. He dialed Superhero James, his best friend from his days at the Superhero Academy.

"James, it's Melvin," Melvin said.

"Buddy!" James was the superhero in charge of Atlanta and hadn't seen Melvin since the Superhero Convention in Las Vegas. "What's up?"

"Trouble is brewing," Melvin said. "Feels like bigger-than-normal trouble. I was wondering if you sensed it, too."

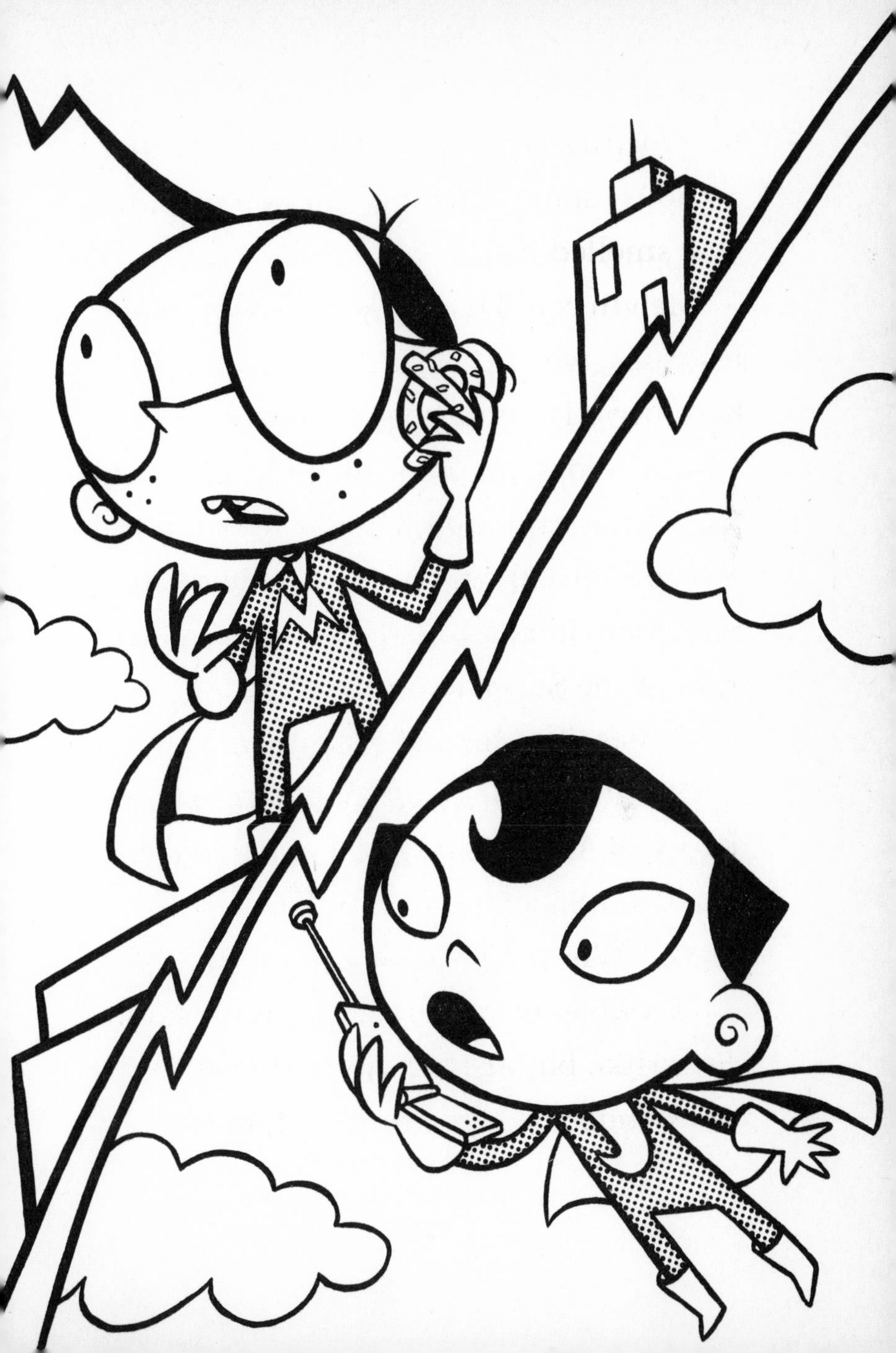

"Hmm, now that you mention it, I do feel something. I thought maybe I was imagining it."

All the graduates of the Superhero Academy could sense evil a mile away. In this case, it seemed that Melvin and James could sense it when it was still millions of miles away.

"Better call Margaret and patch her in," James suggested. They'd known Superhero Margaret at the academy, too. The trio had been best friends ever since.

"Right." Melvin dialed Margaret's number. A few seconds later her voice came through.

"Superhero Margaret, villain thumper with a smile."

"Margaret, it's Melvin."

14

"And James."

A superhero conference call was a very cool thing! It impresses the narrator, anyway. But back to our story.

"Hey, Melvin and James. Can you hold on a second?" Her voice moved away from the phone. "Not so fast!"

Thump!

"Ah . . . that felt good. There's nothing like catching bad guys. What's up?"

"Trouble is heading our way," Melvin said. "Can you feel it?"

"Wow . . . now that you mention it, I think I do. I thought it was heartburn, but trouble brewing makes more sense. Cool! I don't have to go to the doctor." Margaret hated going to the doctor almost as much as she hated bad guys.

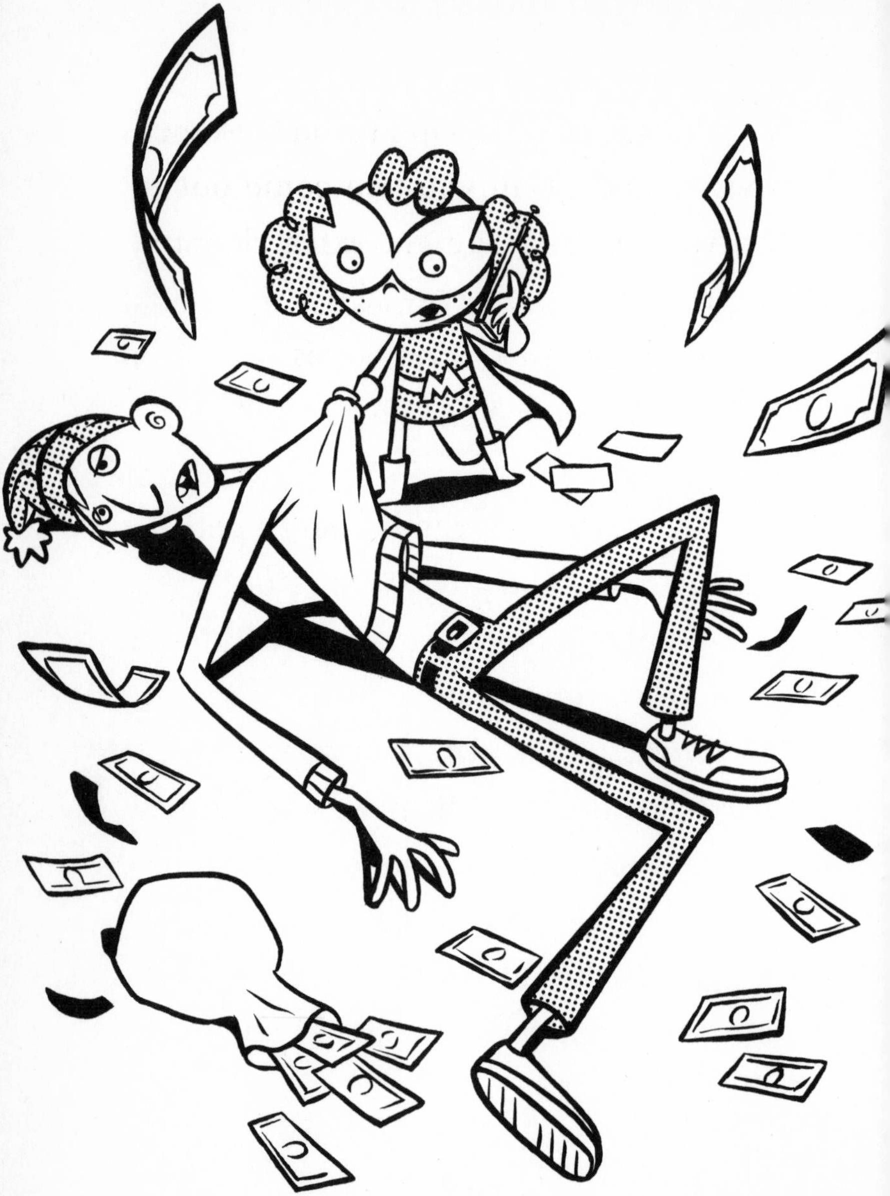

Almost.

"We may have to team up on this one," Melvin said. "Can you two come out to the West Coast? I've got extra sleeping bags."

"I'm on my way," said James.

"Me too," added Margaret.

SUPERHEROES ON PATROL

They weren't the best Zig Newtons Monkey Wrench had ever tasted, but he kept quiet about it. He didn't want to hurt Shoe's feelings. Besides, he had other things on his minds. Their spaceship was getting closer and closer to planet Earth. He couldn't wait to see Earthlings up close. He had seen them plenty of times in books and on video in science class, but seeing them in person would be a first for him.

"Do you think it's true what they say about humans?" Elbow asked, finishing the last of the Zig Newtons. "That they have only one brain?"

"Think so," said Monkey Wrench.

"And they have only two eyes!" Shoe shook his head in disbelief. "I cannot imagine . . . you could read only one book at a time. And what are those things they use to move about?"

"Legs."

"That's right—legs. How interesting."

While the aliens were getting closer to carrying out their sinister plan, Melvin Beederman was meeting with his side-kick, Candace Brinkwater, at the library. He met her there every day after school to help her with math. Then they saved the world together. This was their arrangement—first homework, then bad-guy thumping. Occasionally, they would kick in some doors to round out the day.

"How are things?" Candace asked.

"Not sure," Melvin said. "Bigger-than-normal trouble might be heading our way. Do you feel it?"

Candace slapped her forehead. "I thought that I ate too many pretzels at lunch. But big trouble makes more sense. What kind of trouble?"

"That's the question we've been asking."

"Who's we?"

"James and Margaret are coming out. Four superheroes are better than two.

Finish your math. They're meeting us at my tree house."

Candace smiled and hurried to finish her math. She'd never been inside Melvin's tree house before, but it was on her to-do list. She had her own bedroom, of course, but Melvin had a *tree house*! Life just wasn't fair.

Outside the library, the partners in uncrime launched themselves. Or at least Candace did. Melvin joined her on the fifth try, after crashing, splatting, thudding, and kabonking. Then they flew to the hilltop where Melvin's tree house stood.

James and Margaret were waiting for them inside. Hugo was busy entertaining the new guests with an episode of *The Adventures of Thunderman* and pretzels.

"Squeak," said Hugo when he saw Melvin and Candace. This either meant "Come and join the party," or "Three's a party; five's a crowd." You never knew with Hugo. Although, Candace did—she was fluent in rat.

But she's not narrating the story, now is she?

It was a mini hugfest as the academy friends were reunited. Then Melvin gestured to his partner in uncrime. "You all remember my sidekick, Candace Brinkwater."

"Of course we do, Melvin. We just worked together in book seven."

"Oh, that's right." Melvin was so bothered by the thought that big trouble

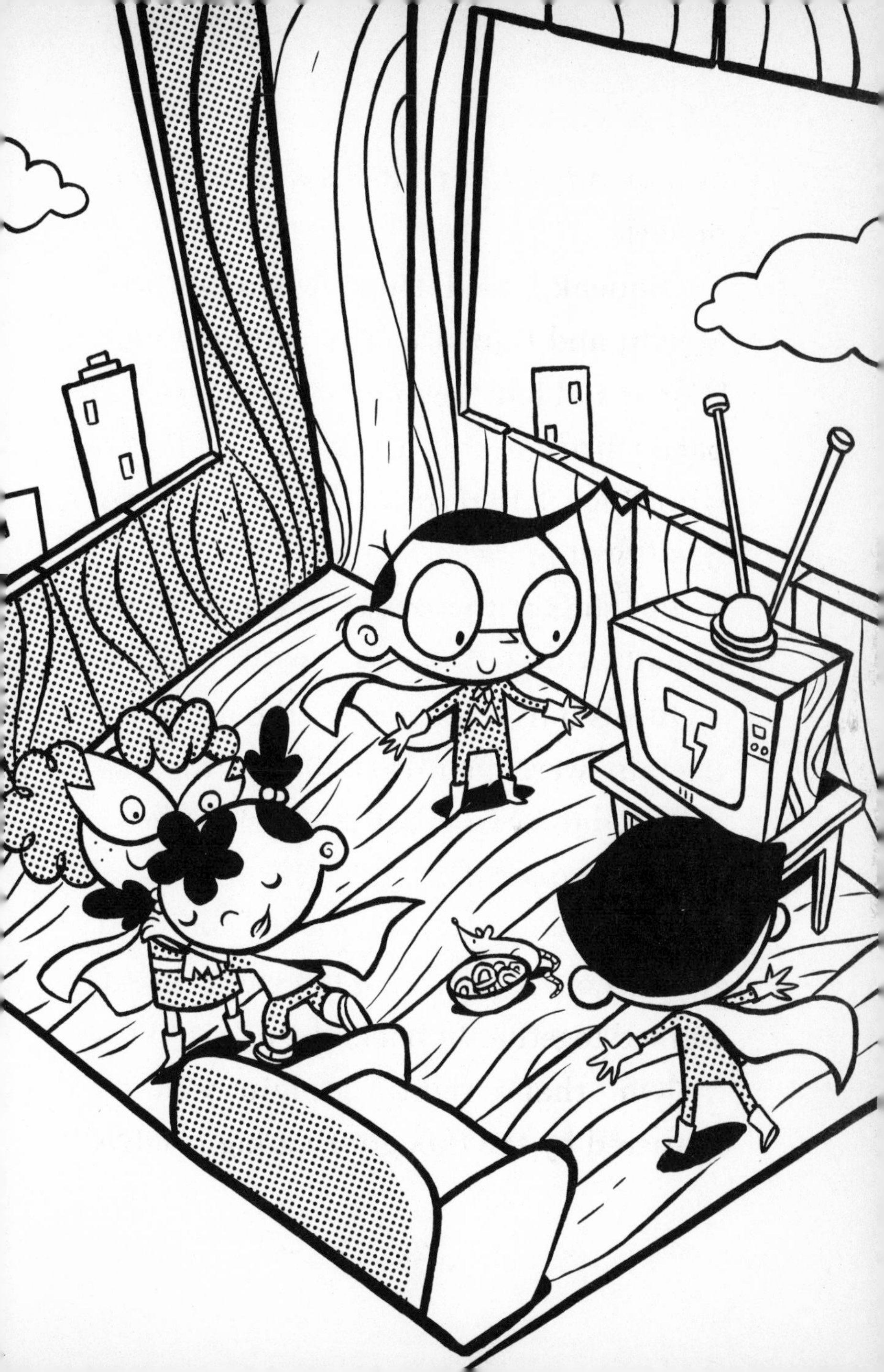

was heading their way that he forgot all about book seven. It happens.

He grabbed a map of the city and spread it out for his three companions. "Where do bad guys like to spend time in this town?"

"Beats me, Melvin," James said. "It's your town."

Melvin turned to his Candace. "Where do you think trouble's mostly likely to come from?"

Candace tapped a finger on the map. "Two places. Lair Hill and beneath the Hollywood sign."

James and Margaret looked confused. Melvin explained. "New lairs are popping up every week in those places. Bad guys galore."

They decided to split up. Margaret and

Candace would patrol Lair Hill, while Melvin and James would check out the hillside below the Hollywood sign. The two pairs of superheroes flew in circles above these areas, looking down for any sign of trouble.

Big mistake! They should have been looking *up*.

MEANWHILE . . .

While Melvin, Candace, Margaret, and James were busy patrolling and looking in the wrong direction, the aliens were getting closer to planet Earth.

"We're getting closer to planet Earth," Monkey Wrench said. He didn't know that he wasn't supposed to repeat what the narrator says. But what can you expect from an alien? Aliens may have two brains, but they don't know much about storytelling.

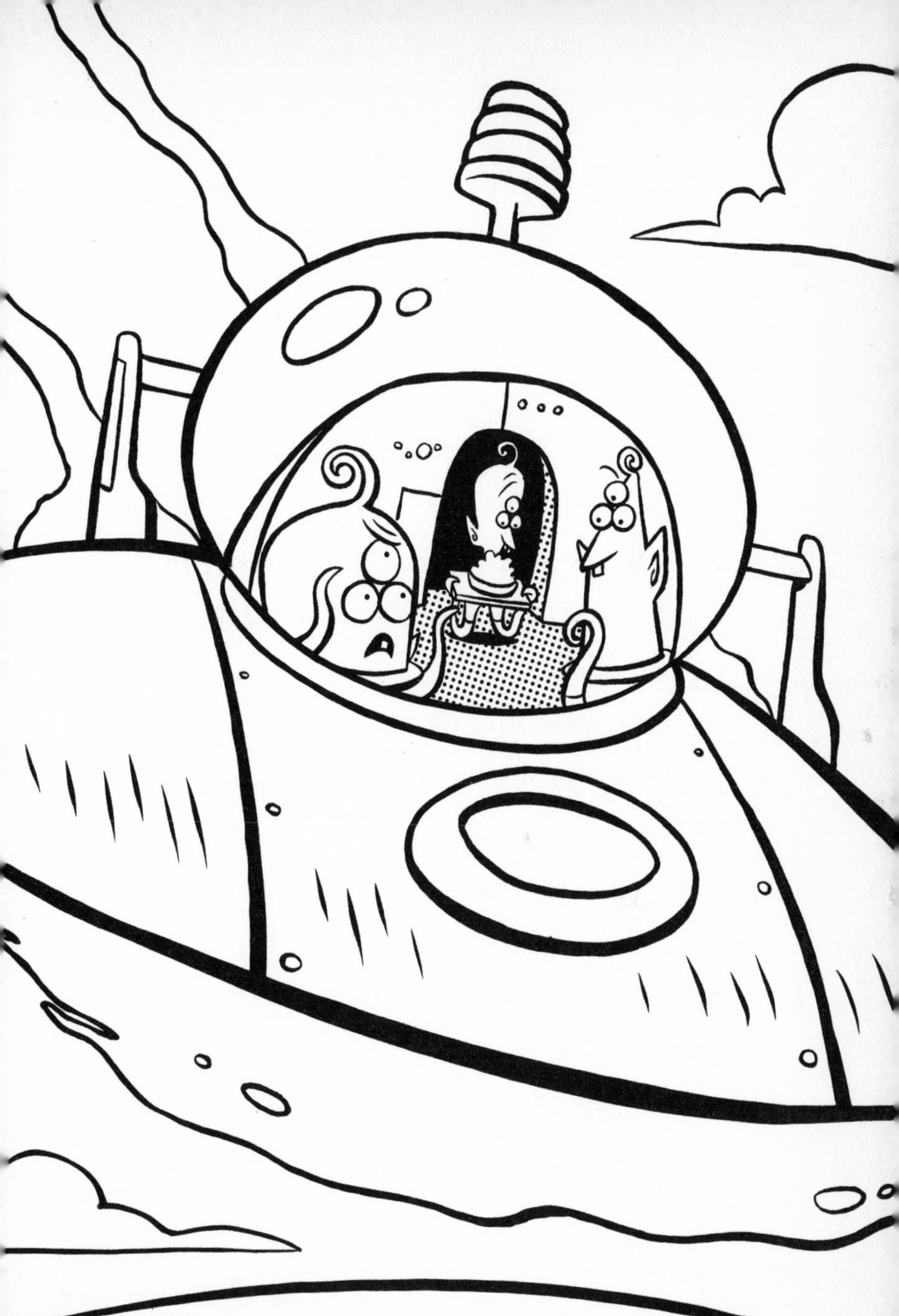

Monkey Wrench and Elbow were at the ship's controls. Shoe was busy in the galley, rustling up something to eat. "Anybody in the mood for rumpkin pie?"

Monkey Wrench and Elbow were too busy to answer.

"We're entering Earth's atmosphere," Monkey Wrench said. "Activate the cloaking device."

"Commencing cloaking activation."

They usually didn't talk to each other with such formal speech. It just looks better in a book to have the leader of a spaceship barking out commands and others responding with words like "commencing."

The problem was that Elbow didn't commence soon enough. . . .

At a nearby air force base, Private Gunther Whusterflap picked up a strange signal on his radar screen. "Sir, some kind of unidentified flying object is entering Earth's atmosphere."

The commanding officer looked over Gunther's shoulder. "Holy alien invasion! Is it my imagination, or are they traveling at Gamma Speed?"

Holy alien invasion, indeed! Wait a minute—how did he know about the aliens? He was just staring at a moving dot on a computer screen. Did he take a peek at the manuscript?

"Oops," said the commanding officer. Peeking at the manuscript was a no-no.

"What are your orders, sir?" asked Private Whusterflap.

"Get the president on the pho—"

Suddenly the blip on the radar screen vanished.

The good news is that the cloaking device worked. Or is that bad news? It depends on whose side you're on. It's good news for the aliens—bad news for the inhabitants of planet Earth.

And it was very bad news for the people of Los Angeles and the four super-heroes who were trying to protect them.

Shoe decided against rumpkin pie and instead made lunarfish sandwiches. He knew Monkey Wrench and Elbow wouldn't say no to lunarfish sandwiches.

He was right. They didn't. They'd need lots of energy to carry out their sinister kidnapping plan. "Thanks, that hit the spot," said Monkey Wrench.

"Yes, thanks," said Elbow.

There's nothing like lunarfish sandwiches before a kidnapping.

WHO DO WE KIDNAP?

Now that Monkey Wrench and Elbow had polished off the lunarfish sandwiches and let out a few satisfying burps, they had the energy to put the pedal to the metal . . . or to push that little lever thingy forward. In any case, the spaceship picked up speed and raced through space toward Earth . . . and closer to one particular city in Southern California.

"Los Angeles, dead ahead." In addition

to using words such as "commencing," Elbow thought it would be a good idea to say things like "dead ahead," which, of course, also look good in a book.

The spaceship was still cloaked. It was invisible to the naked human eye. And let's be honest, most human eyes are naked. But that didn't mean it was silent. Well, the engine was, but not the wind it caused by moving at Gamma Speed.

The ship came in low over the ocean surface, causing twenty-five-foot waves from Malibu to the Ventura County Line.

This is what you call surf's up. This is what you call excellent conditions for hanging ten. This is what you call a good excuse for leaving work early and heading to the beach. This is what you call—

Please stand By:

The Narrator Just Left
Work Early and Is
Heading to the Beach

Where were we? Oh, yes—the cloaked spaceship was moving across the ocean, creating some pretty good waves for local surfers. And they weren't too shabby for local narrators.

"Where do we set this puppy down?" asked Elbow, referring to the spaceship.

"Why not the beach?" Monkey Wrench said.

Yes, why not? They could create more waves so that people could take time off work. And so, just south of Malibu, the cloaked spaceship came to a stop. A few minutes later three aliens appeared, after they finished the last of the lunarfish sandwiches.

It was a crowded day at the beach—

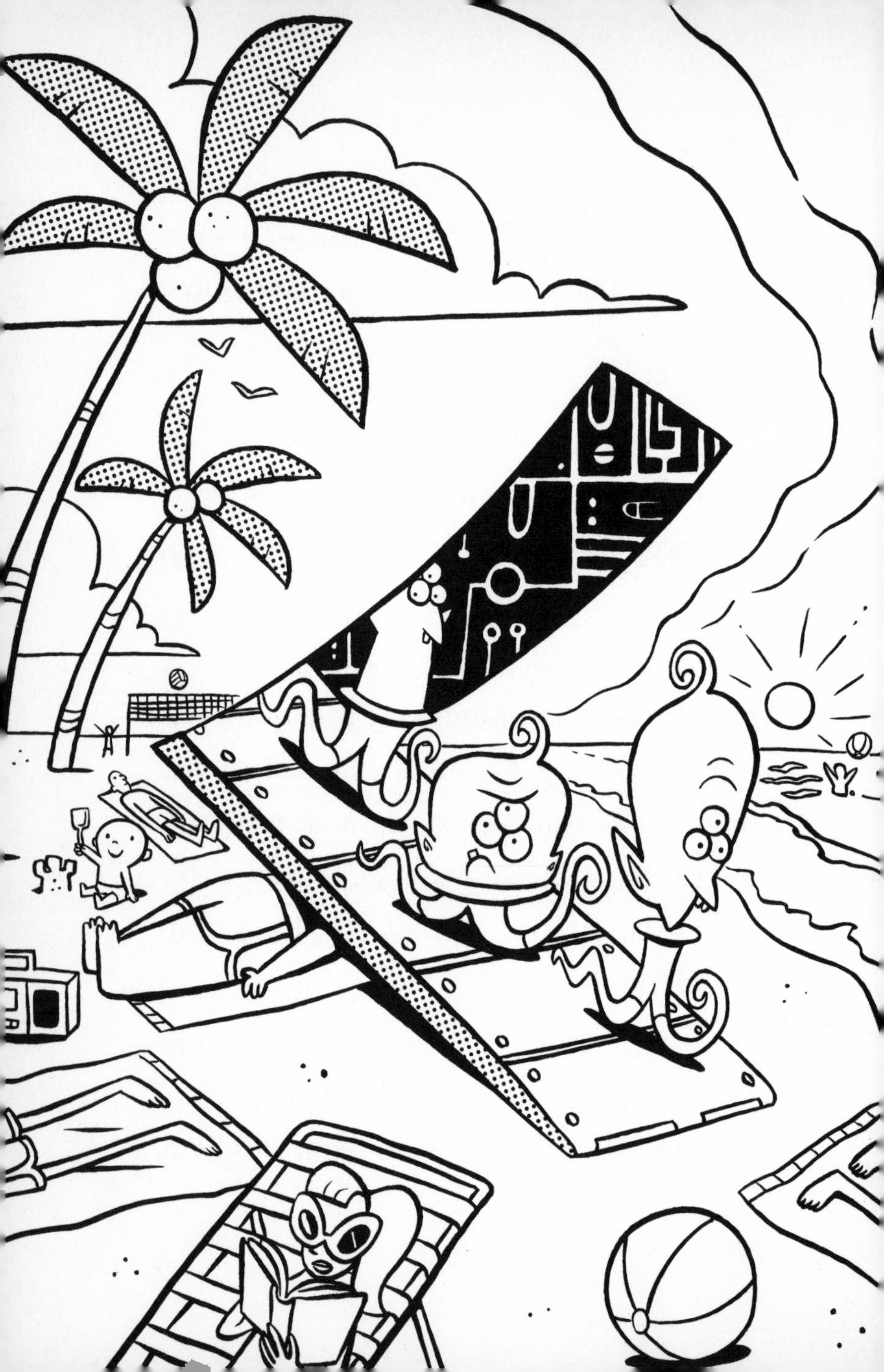

people were sunning themselves, playing volleyball, splashing in the water.

"How do we choose?" asked Monkey Wrench.

Elbow shook his head. "I don't know. So many victims, so little time."

He was only half right. True, there were lots of potential kidnap victims. But they weren't exactly in a hurry to choose.

"Let's head into the city and see what we can see," Monkey Wrench suggested.

They did. They went to downtown Los Angeles and began looking around. There were even more people than at the beach. The aliens wandered about, looking for just the right human to capture and bring back with them to their planet. Not only were there too many to choose from, but each one was different—fat, skinny, old, young, cute, ugly, pimpled, nonpimpled.

"Holy I-can't-make-up-my-mind!" Monkey Wrench said. "This isn't going to be easy."

Holy can't-make-up-his-mind, indeed! What a whiner! Aliens!

Not only was it difficult for the three aliens to decide who to kidnap, it was even harder to agree on someone.

"How about that one?" Shoe would suggest, pointing to a man on a bicycle.

"Nah," Monkey Wrench said. "Too fat."

"Nah," Elbow said. "Too ugly." This was one of Elbow's pet peeves. He hated ugly humans. And ugly aliens, for that matter. But let's be honest—Elbow himself wasn't exactly a looker!

"Or that one?"

"Nah."

"Nah."

Everyone was *too* something. The aliens couldn't agree on anyone. That is, until they wandered over to Lair Hill.

"Look!" said Shoe. "Up in the sky."

"It's a bird," said Elbow.

"It's a plane," added Monkey Wrench. "It's . . . what is it?"

It was Candace and Margaret, that's what. And the aliens came to an agreement, right there on Bad Guy Boulevard, which runs into Sinister Street and parallel to Devious Drive. "Let's capture them and get out of here," Monkey Wrench said.

"Yes, let's," said Elbow.

"Immediately," said Shoe. "Sooner if possible."

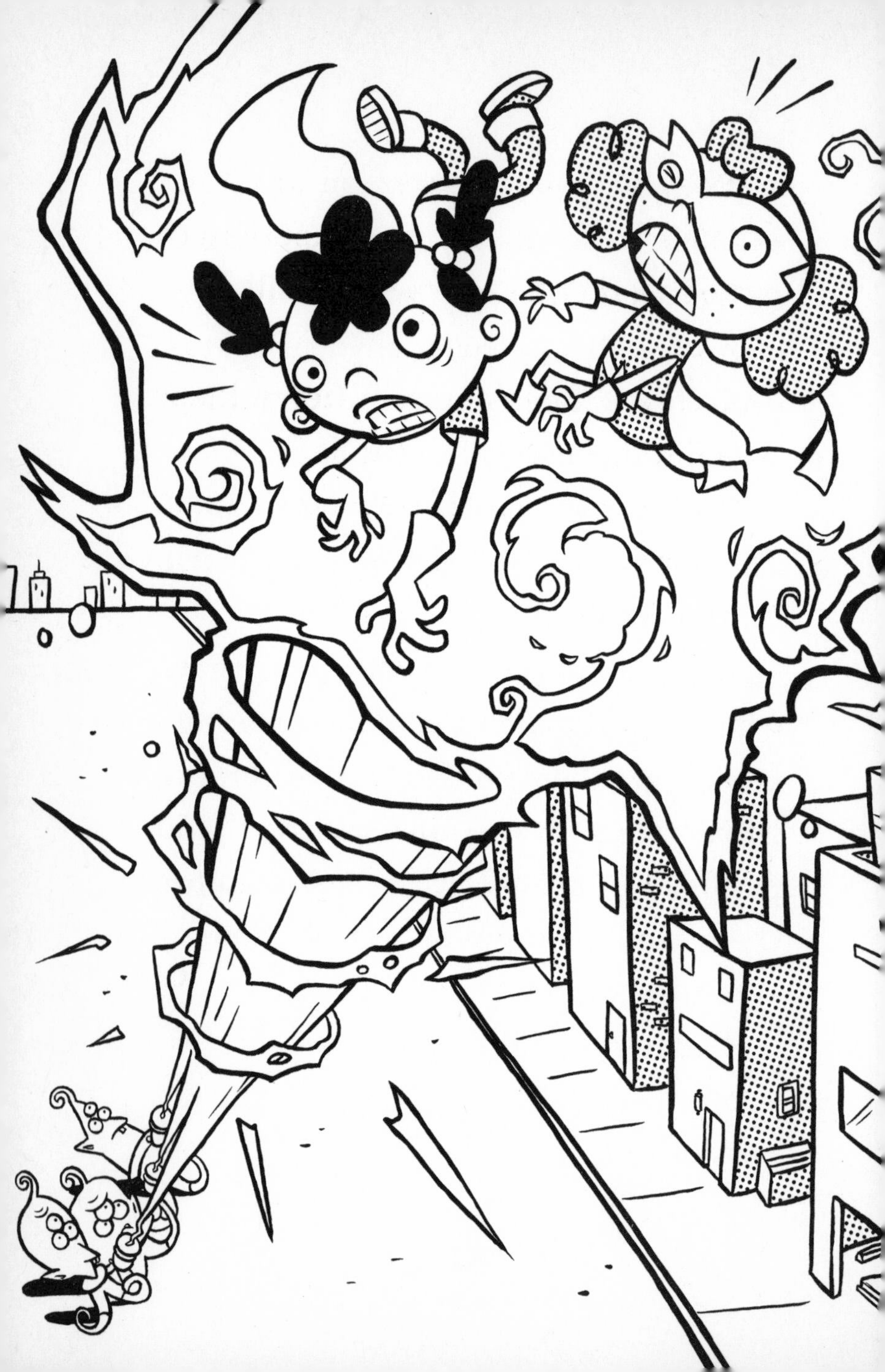

They set their phasers on STUN and pointed them at the two superheroes patrolling the skies above Lair Hill.

ZAP!

Candace and Margaret never knew what hit them. But they felt it.

The question is, did they *crash, splat, thud,* or *kabonk*?

You decide.

STINKY ALIEN FEET

Melvin was confused—and no, he wasn't working on a nasty math problem. He and James were flying above the Hollywood sign, looking for anything sinister or devious.

"That's funny," Melvin said.

"What is?" James asked.

"I just heard something go *splat*, and I'm still flying."

"It sounded more like *thud* to me."

Melvin and James stopped and were hovering. They listened for more crashing sound effects—or kabonking ones. But all was quiet.

"Maybe we should go and check on Candace and Margaret," suggested Melvin.

Yes, Melvin, stop having this mid-air conversation and get moving.

Superheroes!

And so Melvin and James stopped patrolling the air above the Hollywood sign and headed to Lair Hill. Little did they know that they were already too late.

"What if something happened to them?" James said as they streaked across the sky. "What if we're already too late?"

James didn't know he wasn't supposed

to repeat what the narrator said. He'd only been in a few Melvin Beederman books, while Melvin had been in, like, *ALL* of them.

While Melvin and James were high-tailing it over to Lair Hill to check on the girls, Candace and Margaret were picking themselves up off the ground. Or at least they were trying to. They'd not only been shot out of the sky; they'd been stunned.

"Can you move, Candace?" Margaret asked.

"Only my mouth. Wait a second—my eyelids seem to be working."

"Poor Melvin. Now I know what it means to go *splat*."

"Don't you mean *thud*?"

"Whatever."

Yes, girls, whatever. Can't you see those aliens coming your way?

The aliens were getting closer and closer.

"What do we do?" Candace asked, still unable to move.

"Not sure," Margaret replied. "My guess is we won't be able to blink them to death."

Indeed they wouldn't. There was nothing they could do but wait—and scream!

"Shut them up," Monkey Wrench said.

He and the other aliens reached the girls and did just that. They gagged them, using Elbow's socks. If you think humans have stinky feet, you should get a whiff of alien feet. Your nose will never be the same.

But, of course, they didn't gag the girls in time. Their screams still went forth and reached the ears of Melvin and James, who were racing to the rescue.

The problem was, the aliens had a huge head start.

FOLLOW THAT SMELL!

Melvin and James arrived at Lair Hill. The girls were nowhere in sight.

They searched the area. There was no sign of Candace and Margaret. But something smelled terrible—worse than a rotting elephant on a hot day, worse than flaming cow poop, worse than school cafeteria food. Worse than—

James suddenly dropped from the sky, holding his stomach.

Melvin landed beside him. "What's the matter with you?"

"That narrator is grossing me out."

Melvin looked up and yelled, "Enough already!"

Sorry, boys.

"What should we do?" James asked.

"Follow that smell."

James's eyes began to water. "I was afraid you'd say that."

It was a good thing they had super-senstive noses. Okay, maybe it was a bad thing. Still, it helped them stay on track. The your-nose-will-never-be-the-same smell seemed to be leading them to the beach, which was fine with Melvin and James. They had heard about the twenty-five-foot waves. They'd also heard about people taking off early from work— including a certain narrator!

Meanwhile, the bad guys . . . uh . . . aliens arrived at the beach. "Does anyone know where we left the spaceship?" Shoe asked.

"We'll find it when we uncloak." It was a rule on their planet that you had to uncloak before entering your vehicle. Actually, it wasn't a rule; it just made it a lot easier to find the door.

Monkey Wrench pulled out a remote control device and pressed a button. At the end of the street, their spaceship suddenly appeared.

"There it is," Elbow said. He and the others started in that direction.

They weren't the only ones who saw it. A group of beachgoers gathered around.

"Holy spaceship-on-the-beach!" one man said. "This is awesome." He was a surfer, and surfers always used words like "awesome."

Holy spaceship-on-the-beach, indeed! But it wasn't all that awesome. It was a spaceship version of an economy car—30 million miles to the gallon.

The aliens arrived, dragging the stunned superheroes. The onlookers were also stunned, but in a different way. "Hey, isn't that Candace Brinkwater?" said the surfer. He'd seen her picture in the newspaper, along with Melvin Beederman's photo.

Candace, of course, couldn't answer. She was gagged with an alien sock and was practically unconscious from the smell—and the taste.

The aliens threw the girls inside. "Let's get out of here," said Monkey Wrench.

"Yes, let's," said Elbow. "Immediately."

"Sooner if possible," added Shoe. Earth was a nice place to visit, but he wouldn't want to live there.

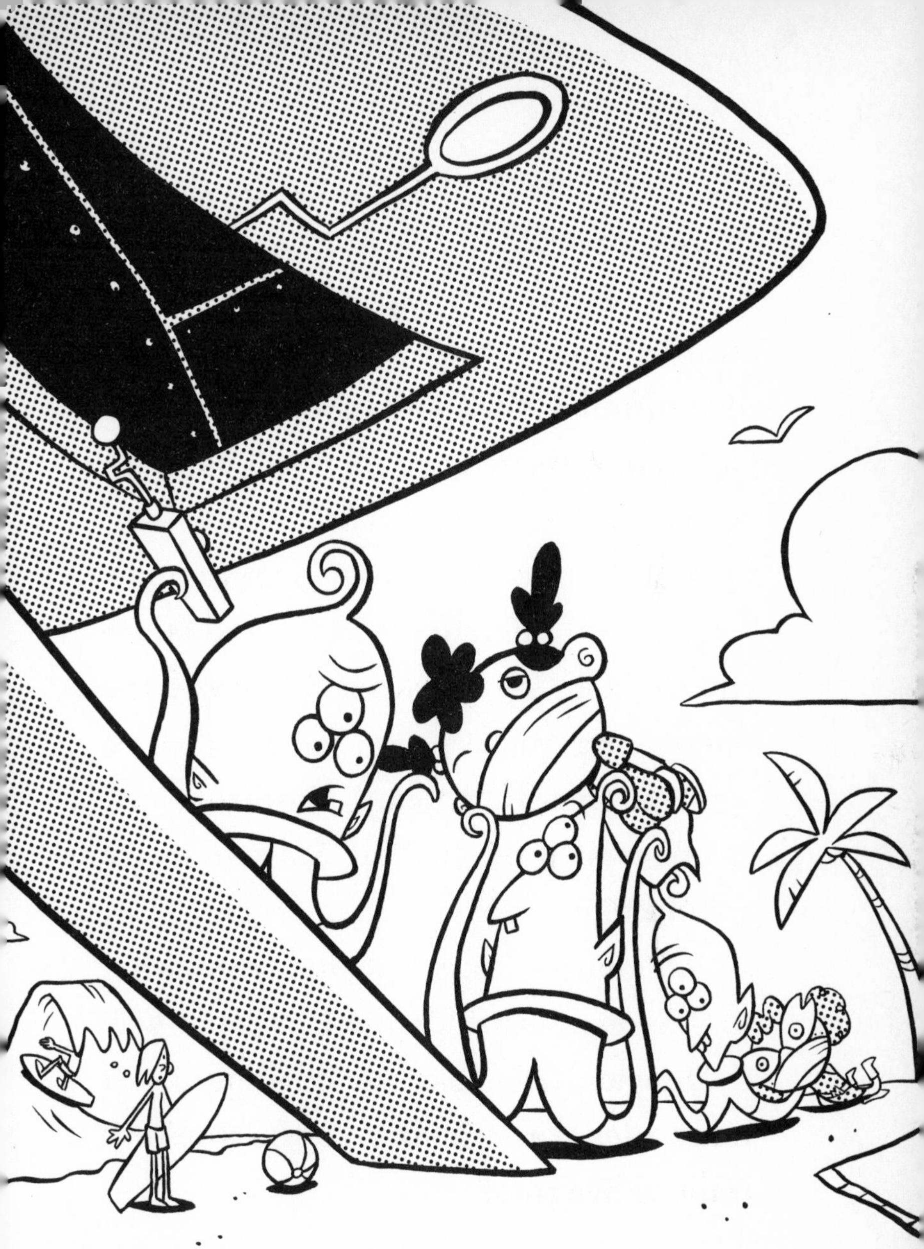

HOLY DISAPPEARING-SPACESHIP!

"Not so fast!" Melvin said as he and James raced along city streets, following the nasty alien smell.

"What do you mean?" James asked. "Don't you want to find Margaret and Candace?"

"Of course. I was just practicing what to say once we find them." Most likely there were bad guys involved, and you had to say the right thing. It was part of the Superhero's Code.

It was a good thing that Melvin and James were as fast as a speeding bullet. They arrived at the beach just in time. Just in the nick of time, to be exact. They saw what looked liked aliens tossing Candace and Margaret into some kind of spaceship—an economy model, but still a spaceship.

"So *that's* what alien underwear looks like," Melvin said. It was even more disgusting than human underwear. It smelled worse, too. Actually, it was the socks that smelled, but Melvin could not tell where the stink was coming from. He was too busy running as fast as a speeding bullet.

The spaceship was surrounded by people who were saying things like "awesome" and "gnarly."

Suddenly the spaceship vanished, which, of course, was *really* gnarly.

"Holy disappearing-alien-spaceship!" Melvin said. "Where'd it go?"

"It's still there," James said. "It's just cloaked. Don't you ever watch *Star Trek*?"

Holy disappearing-alien-spaceship, indeed! Melvin was strictly an *Adventures of Thunderman* person. He wasn't all that familiar with cloaking.

"They cloaked because they're getting ready to take off," James said.

Sure enough, right then they heard the engines roar to life.

"Grab hold of something and hang on tight," said Melvin.

They did. They grabbed hold of the invisible spaceship and hung on just as it lifted from the ground.

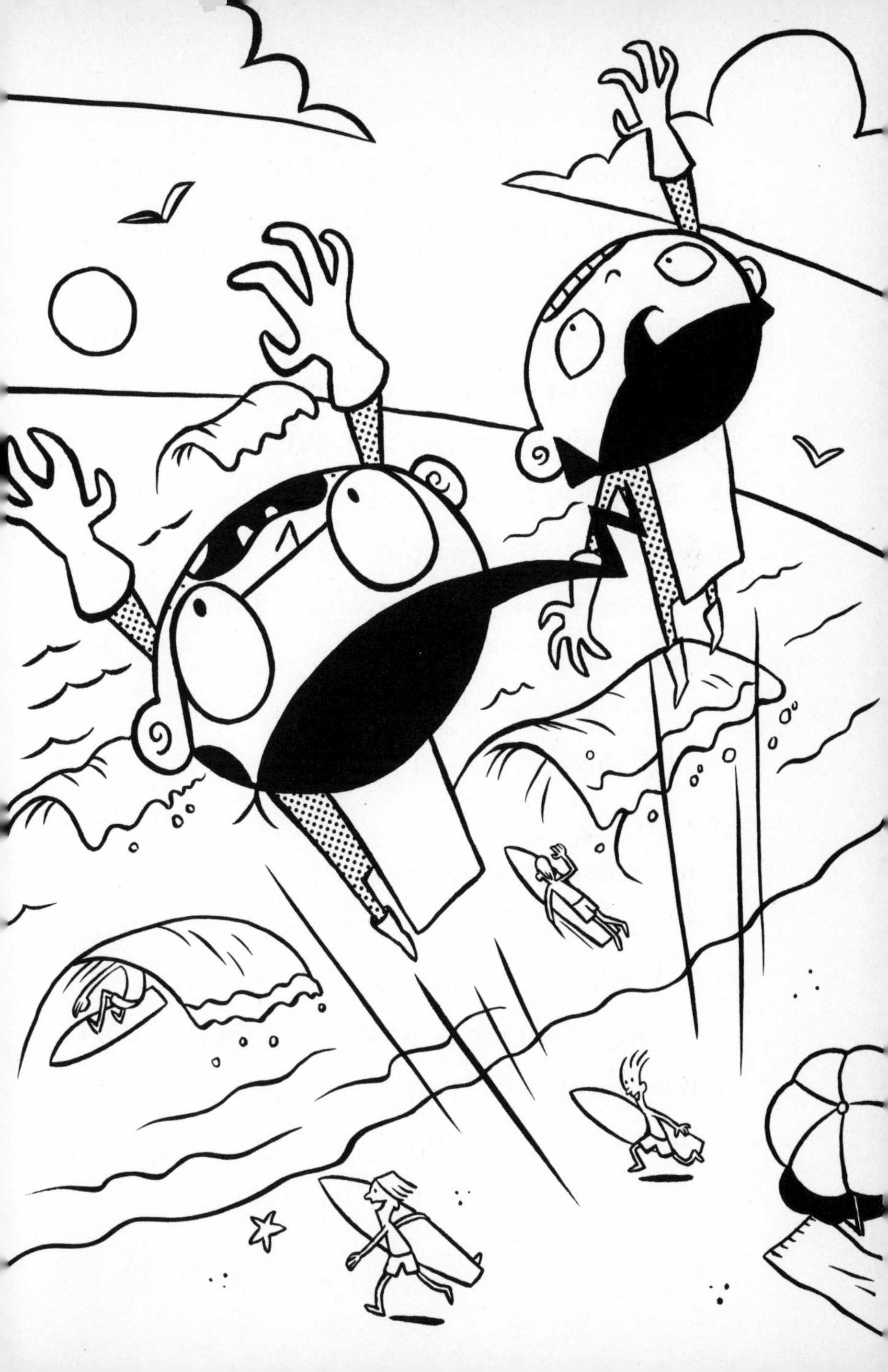

Before they knew it, they were moving at Gamma Speed and creating huge waves, leaving behind cries of "awesome" and "gnarly" as the surfers grabbed their boards and raced for the water.

Gamma Speed was pretty darn fast. Melvin and James soon found themselves traveling through outer space.

"Can I ask you something, Melvin?" James said.

"Shoot."

"We're in outer space, right?"

"Yep."

"So how are we able to breathe?"

Melvin looked at his friend. "The same way Superman does. Besides, haven't you ever heard of suspension of disbelief?"

"What?"

"Never mind. Let's get on with the story."

Yes, boys, let's.

As the two superheroes sped along on the invisible spaceship, Melvin began to feel around for a seam in the metal surface, something he could pry open. What he found was even better—a door handle. At least it felt like one. In a few seconds the spaceship uncloaked. It was some kind of hatch, all right. Melvin tugged with all his might and ripped it from its hinges.

He tossed it to the side. "James, follow me. I found a way in."

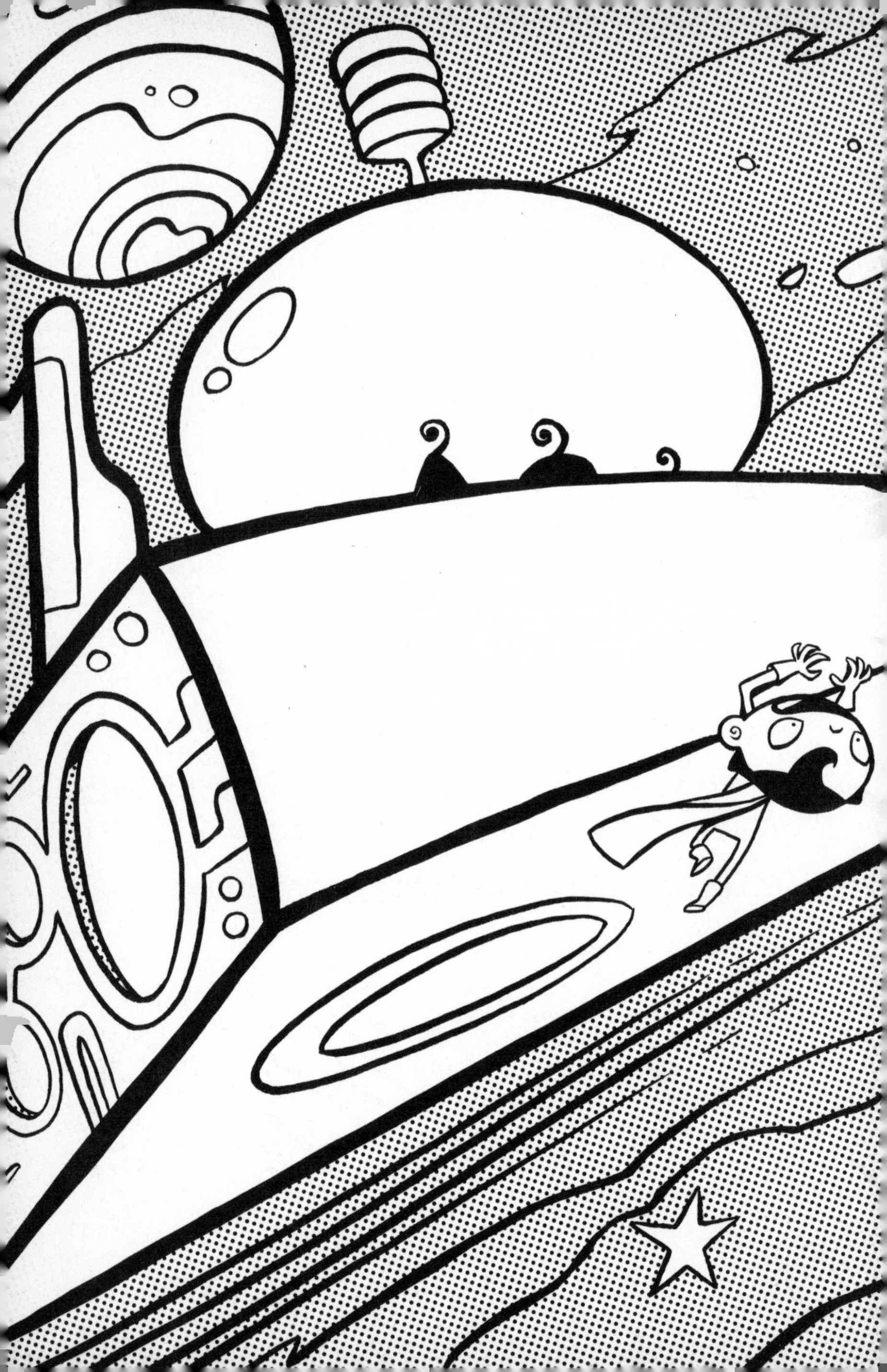

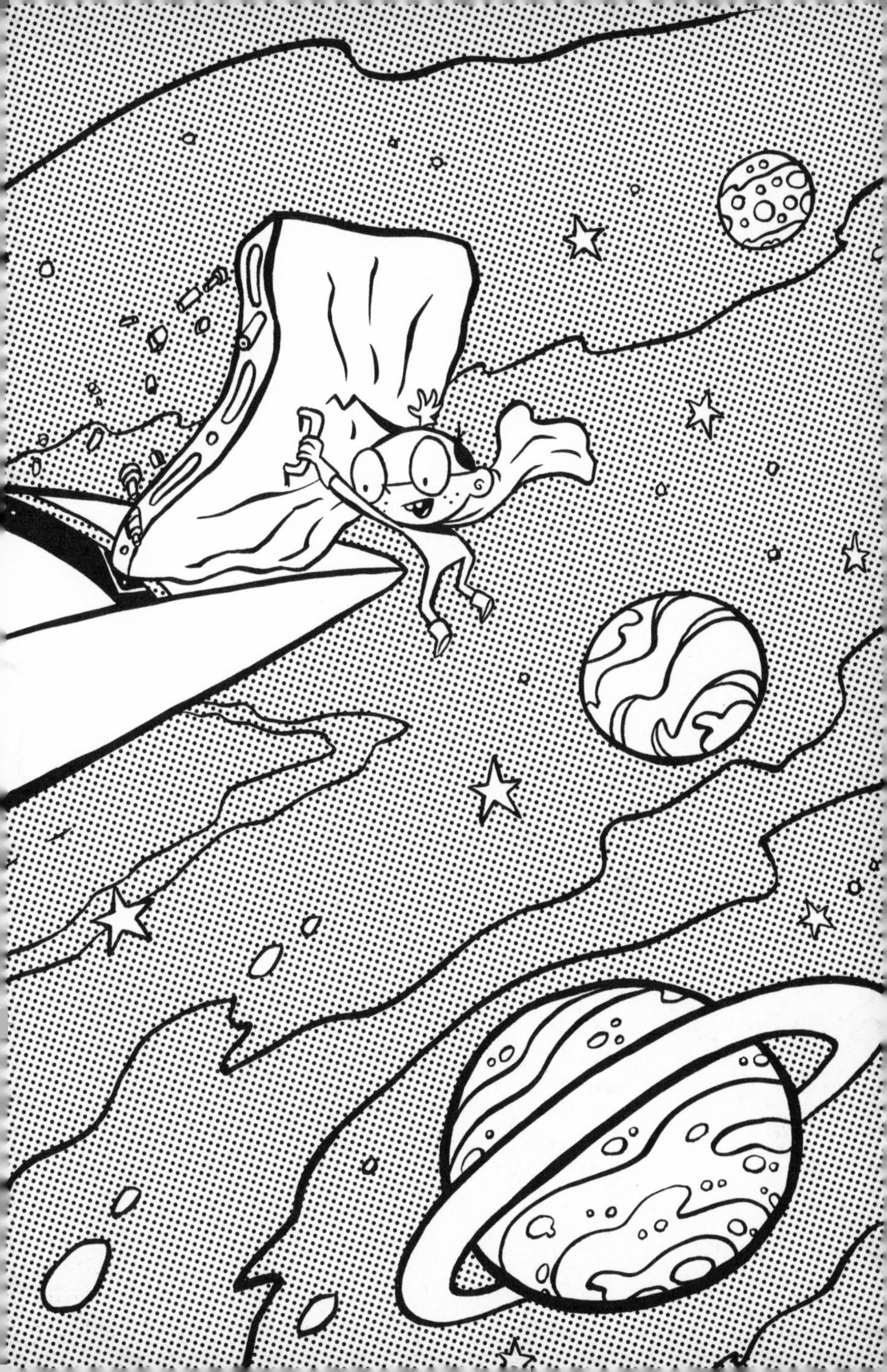

ALIEN ROCK AND ROLL

The spaceship was rocking. No, it wasn't passing through an asteroid field. Elbow had cranked up the volume on the stereo, and now The Space Aliens—not the ones who kidnapped Candace and Margaret— were demonstrating the very latest in intergalactic rock and roll. They weren't exactly The Grateful Fred, but what do you expect from a planet called Dork? Then again, they weren't bad.

It was a good thing that Elbow had

turned up the music, because when Melvin ripped open the hatch, no one inside heard the noise. Not even Candace and Margaret. They were both pretty upset about being kidnapped and being gagged with smelly alien socks, but they both had to admit The Space Aliens had talent. In fact, Margaret was snapping her fingers.

Candace saw this and realized that the stun gun had worn off. "Psst, Margaret, it's time to make our move."

The problem was, of course, *what* move would they make? They were in outer space, for crying out loud! Neither of them knew how to fly a spaceship, or how to find Earth again. They were also inside some kind of glass cage with no door.

"That's weird," Margaret said.

"What is?" Candace asked.

"We're in this glass enclosure with no door. How are we able to breathe?"

"Haven't you ever heard of suspending your disbelief?"

"What?"

"Never mind. Let's get out of here." Candace threw herself against the glass. Nothing happened. She kicked it. No change. She tried her famous karate chop. The glass stayed intact.

"We're in trouble," Candace said with a worried look. "Those were three of my best moves." She was an expert at breaking down doors and crashing through walls, but this time they didn't work.

"Two superheroes are better than

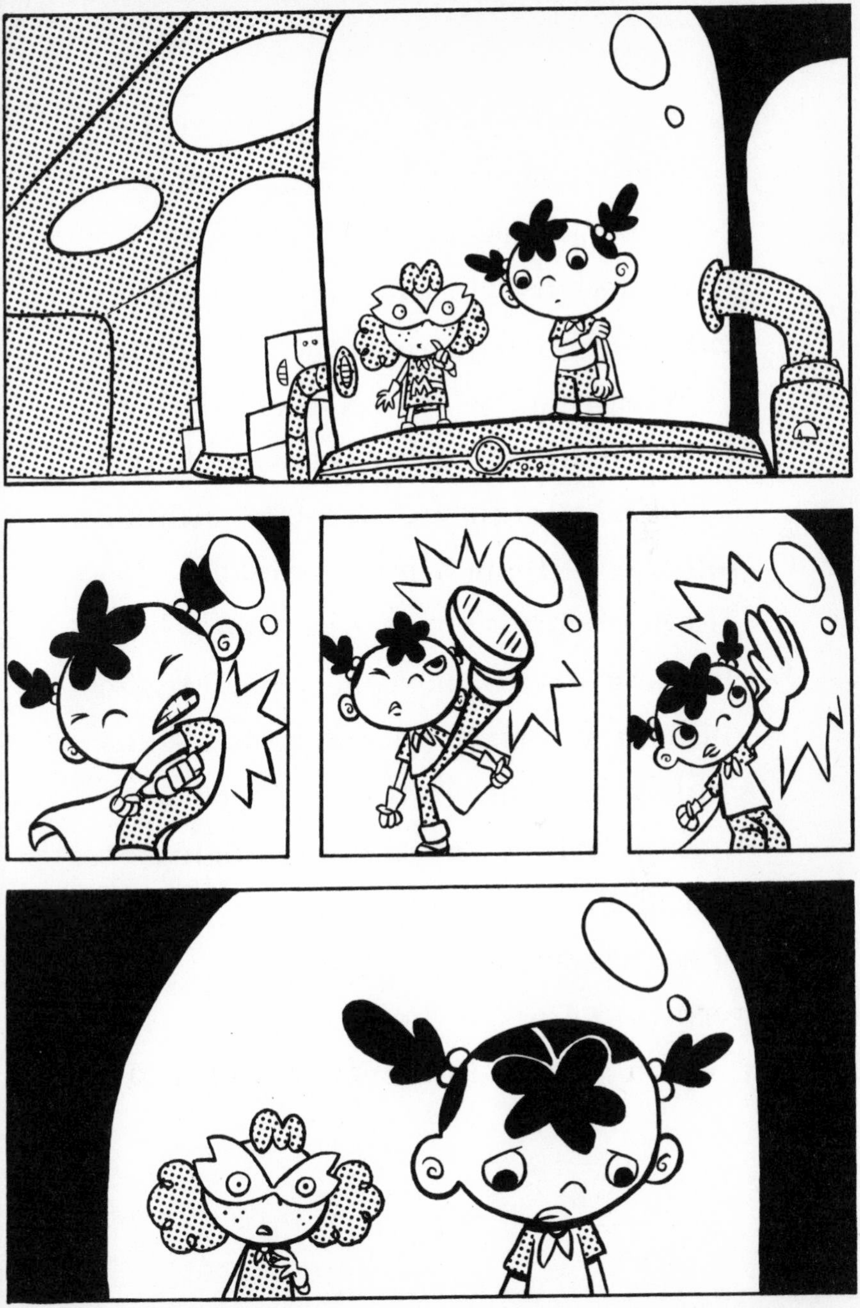

one," Margaret said, getting to her feet. "Let's try it again. On three . . . *THREE!*"

Two superheroes are indeed better than one, but in this case it wasn't enough to break through the alien glass.

"Now what?" Margaret asked.

"I wish Melvin and James were here."

The boys, of course, were a few million miles closer than Candace thought.

After ripping off the door and climbing inside the spaceship, Melvin and James found themselves in some kind of transition room. There were strange-looking space suits hanging on hooks. On the far wall there was a door with a window.

Melvin crossed the room and peered through it. Then he carefully opened the door and stepped out, waving for James to follow. They stood in a long hallway with many doors. The music was loud and Melvin began snapping his fingers. He wondered if The Space Aliens ever toured Earth. They were almost as good as The Grateful Fred. Almost.

"Now to find the girls," Melvin said.

They crept down the hall toward the music. And that's when they smelled it–stinky alien feet! Someone, or some*thing*, was coming their way.

"Quick!" Melvin said, pointing to the room they'd just come from. "Back in there—hide."

They sprinted down the hall to the transition room and closed the door behind them. The smell got worse—

closer, stinkier, like a rotting alien corpse on a hot day, like moldy lunarfish sandwiches, like—

"Enough already!" Melvin said.

Some people have no patience for quality description.

"Now what?" James asked.

Melvin pointed to the space suits hanging on the wall. "There!" It was the only place to hide. They climbed into the suits . . . just in time. Just in the nick of time, to be exact.

An alien face appeared in the window. Then the door swung open and there stood Monkey Wrench.

Melvin held his breath. So did James.

ZAP!

Melvin didn't move a muscle. He peered out of the space-suit helmet, hoping Monkey Wrench wouldn't look to the side, where Melvin was in plain view. So was James. Both superheroes stayed completely still.

Monkey Wrench stood in the room a few minutes, examining the damage of the torn-off hatch. He shook his head, muttered something to himself, then turned and went back into the hall.

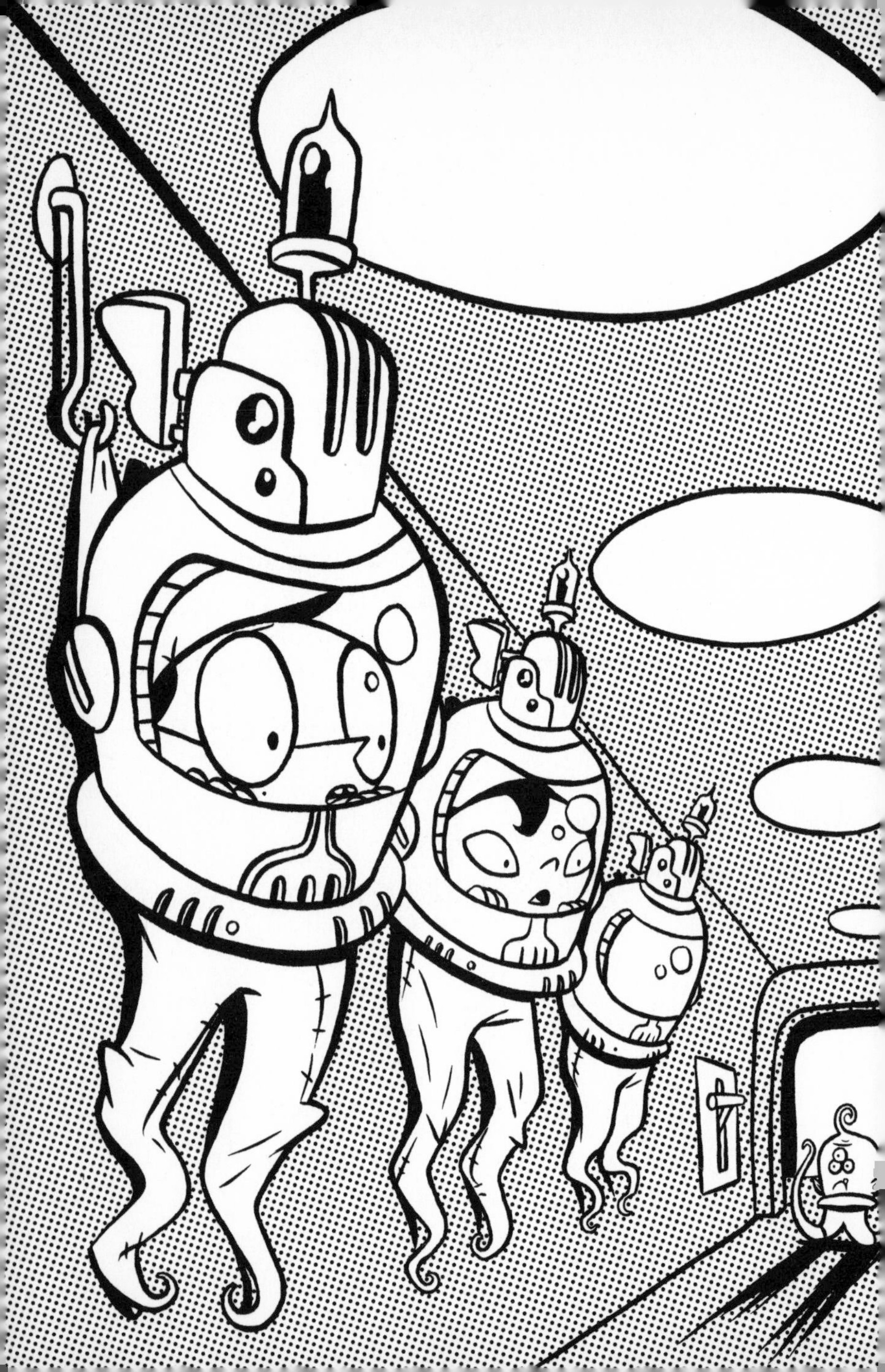

When he closed the door behind him, Melvin and James heard it lock.

They climbed out of the space suits. "Curses!" James said. "Now what?"

Melvin gave him a look. "Curses? Only the bad guys say curses."

"I'm in outer space. I can't think straight. What are we going to do? We're locked in."

"We're superheroes," Melvin said. "Since when is a locked door a problem?"

"Good point."

Melvin put an ear to the door, listening for any sign of the alien. James put his nose to the door for the same reason. The Space Aliens were still rocking out. *Good,* thought Melvin. *No one will hear me rip the door open.* Ripping doors open was almost as much fun as kicking them in.

Almost.

Melvin and James tiptoed down the hall and looked around the corner. No sign of any nonhumans. There was also no sign of Candace and Margaret. The boys kept moving forward, checking doors. Most of them were locked. There was no sense in breaking them down—yet—not until they located the girls.

Melvin and James stopped suddenly. They heard voices.

They were coming from the flight deck up ahead, or whatever you call the control room of a spaceship. Hey, maybe control room! Melvin and James peered in and saw three aliens. They'd seen the one called Monkey Wrench before. He was obviously the leader. He was barking out commands—and meowing a few.

"Elbow, better go check on our captives," he said. "Shoe, second star on the right, straight on till morning."

"Ahem," Shoe said. "Wrong story, Monkey Wrench."

"Oops."

Elbow crossed the flight deck to an open doorway and looked inside. He returned and nodded. "They're fine," he said.

Melvin pulled James back into the hallway. "I'm going to check on Candace and Margaret," he whispered. "You stay and watch the aliens. Learn anything you can about how they fly this ship. We'll have to find our way back to Earth eventually."

James nodded. Back at the academy he had been a computer genius. And he was pretty decent at playing video games. If anyone could fly a spaceship, he could.

The three aliens were looking out into space through the huge window that spanned the room. Melvin crawled behind them, army-style. He went through the open door and found the girls. They were inside some kind of glass cage. It had no door at all, no easy way to get in or out, it seemed.

Melvin put a finger to his lips. He wondered why Candace hadn't broken through yet. She was a master at kicking through walls. He placed his hands on the glass and felt around for a seam or a weak spot, but Candace shook her head and mouthed the words, *Can't break through.*

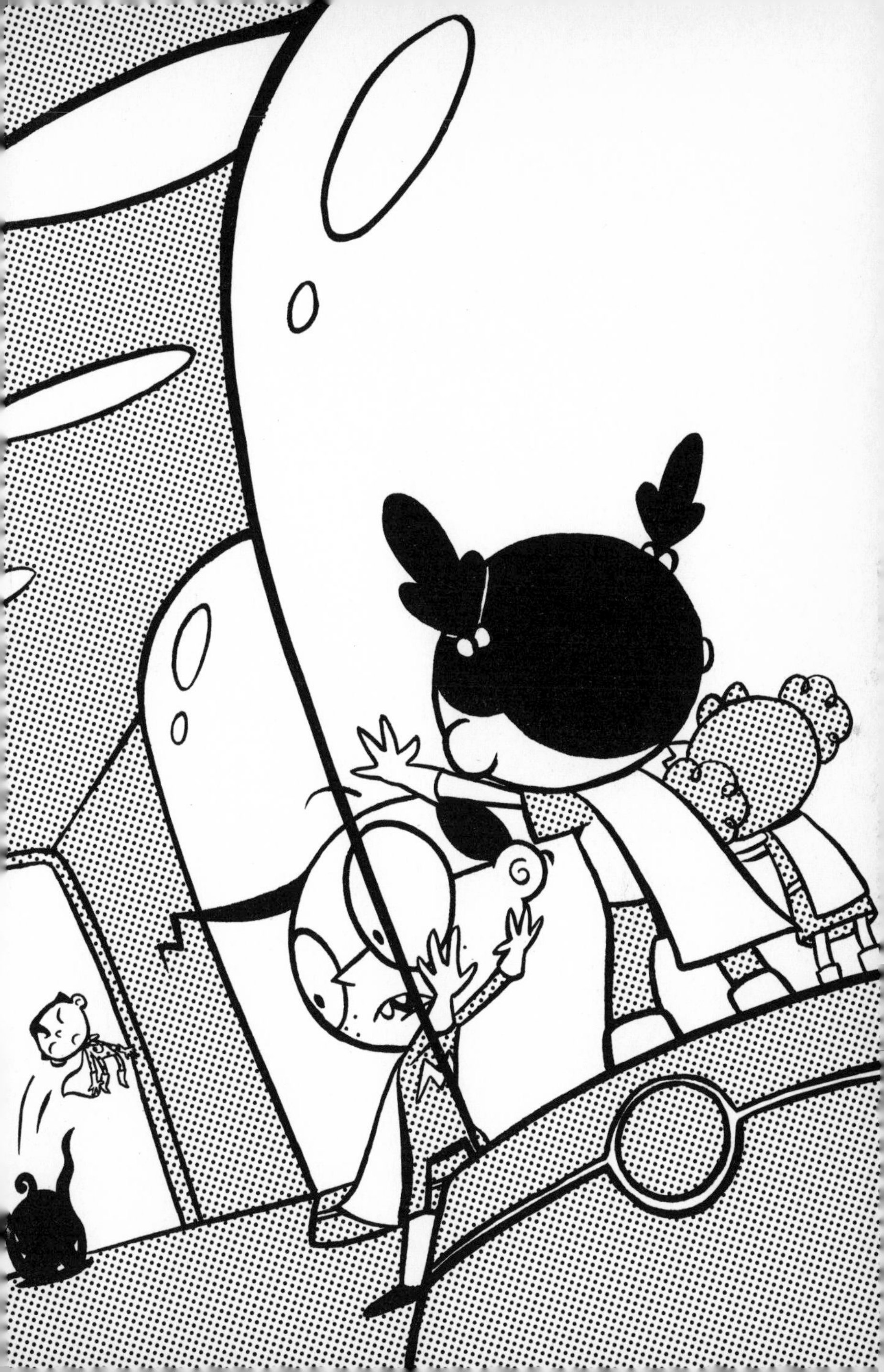

Maybe two superheroes couldn't break through, but how about four? They'd need James. Melvin turned around to go get him. But James was already there. One of the aliens had tossed him into the room. He lay on the ground, staring up at Melvin, only his eyelids moving.

ZAP!

A second later Melvin found himself lying next to James, looking up at the ceiling. All he could do was blink.

FOUR SUPERHEROES
ARE BETTER THAN TWO

"Why can't I move?" Melvin said, still staring at the ceiling.

"Didn't you hear that *ZAP*?" James replied. "Some kind of stun gun, I'm guessing."

Candace came over. "They captured us the same way. One minute we were patrolling the skies above Lair Hill, the next we were on the ground staring at the clouds. It will wear off soon. You'll be good as new."

"Good as new, but still trapped," Margaret said.

"Any ideas on how to get out of here?"

Melvin was unable to move, but that didn't mean he couldn't *think*. After all, he was known for his noggin power, his ability to think on his feet. He wasn't exactly on his feet at the moment, but he was pretty sure he could do the job from his back.

"You tried breaking through the glass?" Melvin asked.

"Both of us did," Candace explained. "Couldn't even make a dent."

"Maybe four superheroes working together can." It was worth a try at least.

When Melvin and James regained their strength, they tried.

"On three," Melvin said. *"THREE!"*

They threw themselves against the nearest wall. *Crash!*

A few seconds later, Shoe appeared in the doorway. "That's glass from the planet Dork. It's unbreakable." He pointed to a button on the wall of the room—outside the glass cage. "Besides, there's a force field holding it together. You won't get out of there until I push that button."

"Rats," Candace said, shaking a fist. She wanted to say something much worse than "rats." But this is a kids' book.

"How can a planet called Dork invent unbreakable glass?" Melvin grumbled.

Shoe went back to the flight deck, and the four superheroes huddled together, thinking. "Now what?" Margaret asked. "Any ideas?"

"We wait," Melvin said. "We can't

break through this glass. Let's wait until they move us. They'll have to turn off that force field to do it."

It was the only thing Mr. Noggin Power could think of.

You may be wondering—if they are going to do nothing, how is the plot going to move forward? Good question.

The spaceship sped through space at Gamma Speed, which is pretty darn fast for an economy spaceship. It got closer and closer to their destination—planet Dork—stopping only once to refuel at Fast Freddy's Gas Station and Pretzel Barn. If you've never tasted alien pretzels, you haven't lived. They are flavor-packed, delicious, energized morsels, bursting with the aroma of heavenly and yummy—

Suddenly Melvin collapsed onto the floor of the glass room.

"What's wrong?" James asked.

"It's the narrator again."

"Do you want me to tell him enough already?"

"No! I'm loving it. It just makes me hungry."

It made him more than hungry. It also made him miss Hugo, his pet and partner-in-pretzel-eating, who at the moment was millions of miles away.

Or was he?

"Squeak."

Melvin sat up. "Either someone's shoes just squeaked or my favorite rat is nearby."

Actually, it could be an alien rat . . . or alien mouse for that matter. The point is something squeaked, and it sounded an awful lot like Hugo.

The sound came again. "Squeak, squeak."

Melvin began looking at his fellow superheroes' shoes. None of them were making noise. Then—

"Squeakity, squeaker, squeak!" Shoes

may be capable of making a squeak or two, but they couldn't possible make a squeakity or a squeaker. And that meant only one thing.

"Hugo!"

It was Melvin's rat, all right. He had climbed onto Melvin's cape before he and James had set off for the Hollywood sign that morning.

He'd been hiding in the transition room of the spaceship, waiting to make his move.

"Get us out of here, Hugo," Melvin whispered. He sniffed. "And get me one of those pretzels." Melvin's nose knew a good thing when he smelled it.

HUGO TO THE RESCUE

"Squeak, squeak," said Hugo with a twitch of his rat whiskers. This either meant "What's a nice superhero like you doing in a place like this?" or "Can you sing 'Boogie Fever' in the key of G?"

Melvin wasn't sure. He was just glad to see his rat again. Now to make their escape.

The problem was, Hugo was one short rat. And the button that needed to be pushed was halfway up the wall.

"Can you find a way to reach that button?" Melvin asked.

"Squeak," replied Hugo. This meant "I'm on it, big guy." Or maybe it was "Are there any cute rats in the vicinity?" Hugo was always on the lookout for attractive rodents.

No alien rats were around, just four superheroes trapped inside a glass cage. Hugo looked around. Outside the cage there were a couple of cabinets, a picture on the wall, some boxes—

Boxes! Of course! Hugo pushed one of them beneath the button and climbed on top. This got him a little closer, but not close enough. He jumped down and grabbed another box, lifting it over his head. He was pretty strong for a rat. He and Melvin often had push-up contests while watching *The Adventures of Thunderman*—during commercials, of course—and now it was paying off.

Hugo tossed the box on top of the other and climbed up. He reached for the button and—

ZAP!

Hugo found himself staring at the ceiling, unable to move anything but his whiskers.

"Squeak?" he said. This either meant "Why can't I move?" or "I hate when this happens." He sure did.

Shoe walked over and picked up Hugo by the tail. "What do you call it?" he asked his four caped prisoners.

"His name is Hugo," Melvin said. "He's a rat." He was going to say, "He's *MY* rat," but decided the less the aliens knew the better.

Shoe sniffed Hugo. He was tired of Zig Newtons and lunarfish sandwiches. He wondered what a Hugo-on-rye would taste like. He gave the rat another sniff, then looked at Melvin.

"*POISON*," Melvin said. "I wouldn't even touch him if I were you. You might want to wash your hands."

Shoe decided not to risk it. He switched the force field off for only a second, long enough to toss Hugo in with Melvin and the others.

"Nice try, Hugo," Melvin said, petting his rat. "You'll be back to normal in a few minutes."

"Squeak." This probably meant "I'm so glad I'm not a sandwich." But it could have meant "Is it just me, or do those alien pretzels smell terrific?"

They did, but Melvin and his companions had other things to think about. How to escape, for one? Also, how to find the way back to Earth? For now, all they could do was wait.

And so that is exactly what they did— they sat together in the glass cage and waited.

"Anyone know any good knock-knock jokes?" Candace asked. She would have suggested a game of Go Fish if she'd had cards.

Everyone was fresh out knock-knock jokes, it seemed.

The landing on planet Dork wasn't the smoothest in the world. But what do you expect from a bunch of teenage aliens flying an economy spaceship? In a few minutes, Monkey Wrench, Elbow, and Shoe entered the room with the glass cage and turned off the force field.

The three of them had their stun guns out and looked like they weren't afraid to use them. "Try anything and you get zapped," Monkey Wrench said.

Melvin just stood there, staring at their disgusting alien underwear. *Now what?* he thought. Things were getting worse and worse. And he knew exactly who to blame.

The narrator!

WHO'S THAT ALIEN?

They had landed in some kind of alien school yard. There were alien basketball hoops, alien handball courts, alien jungle gyms. It was all very familiar and yet very strange at the same time.

"Get moving," Monkey Wrench said. "And bring along that thing with the tail."

"It's a rat," Shoe said with a little pride. He loved knowing something that

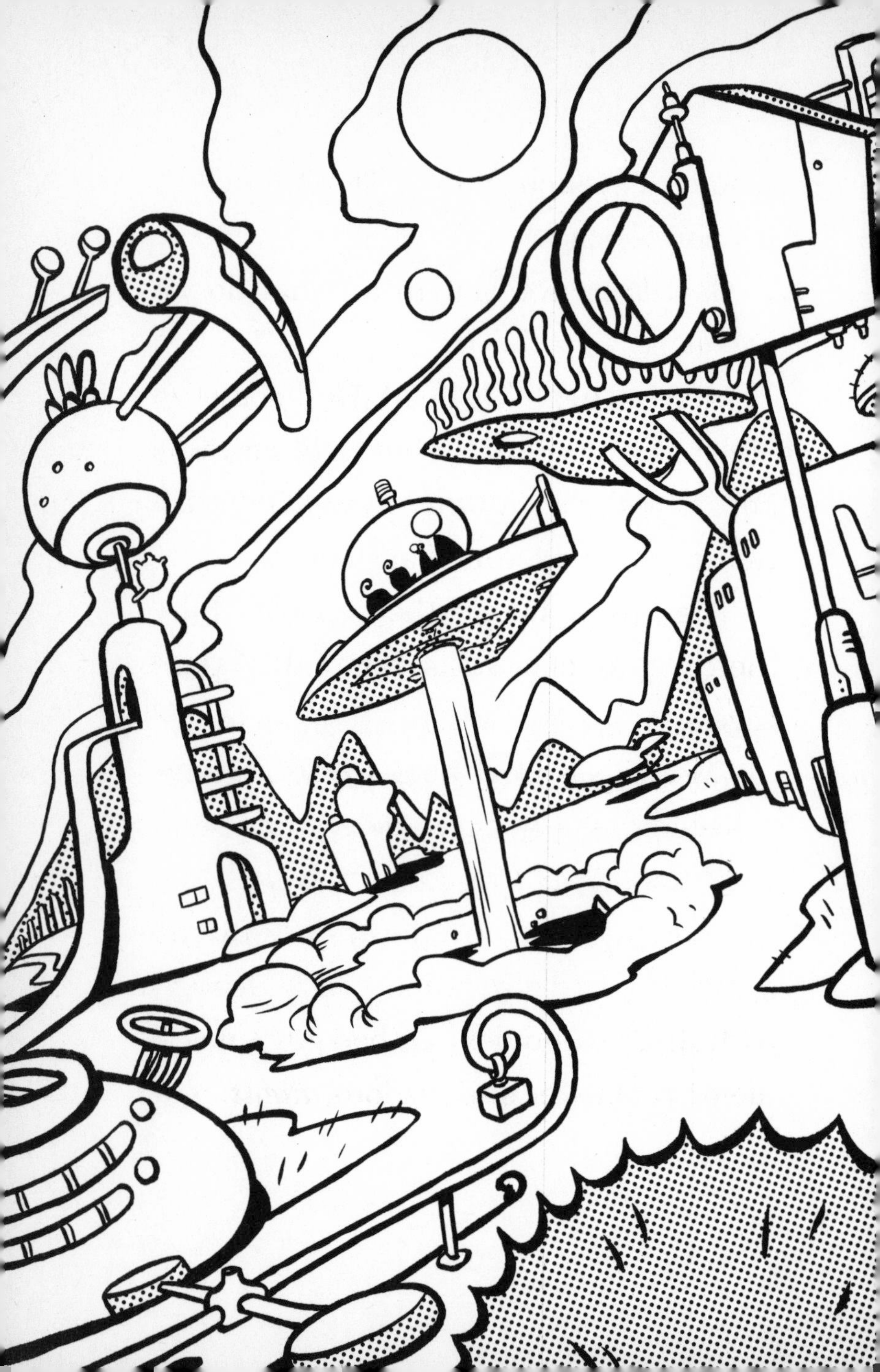

Monkey Wrench didn't. "Don't touch it. It's poisonous."

Candace gave Melvin a "what do we do?" look.

Melvin shook his head. He'd come up with a plan eventually, but right now was not the time to do anything—not with those stun guns aimed at them.

They went inside the school, where there was an enormous room full of glass cages.

"More glass from planet Dork," James whispered. There was nothing worse than glass from planet Dork.

This wasn't going to be easy. But, then again, it never was when you're dealing with sinister and devious bad guys, not to mention sinister and devious *aliens*.

Elbow and Shoe shoved Melvin and company into one of the glass cages. Once again, it was protected by a force field. "Lucky for you, science class does not begin for a couple of hours," Monkey Wrench said. He looked at Elbow and Shoe. "Let's go grab some breakfast."

They left the room, closing the door behind them.

Melvin and his superhero companions suddenly realized they were not alone. Someone was in the cage next to them—a strange, nonhuman someone. Melvin looked at it and said, "Do you know English, by any chance?"

The alien captive shook its head. "No,

but if you hum a few bars I think I can fake it."

Just what Melvin needed, an alien with a sense of humor. But at least he had on clean underwear. Melvin turned his attention back to his own cage. How to break out of unbreakable glass? Wait a minute. Of course! X-ray vision!

"I've got it!"

The alien in the next cage said, "By Jove!"

Melvin pulled out a pen from his pocket and made a single dot on the wall of the cage. "Everyone, focus your x-ray vision of that. This glass can't break, but maybe it can melt." X-ray vision could do more than see through things; it could also be used as a laser.

"On three," Melvin said. *"THREE!"*

The four superheroes aimed their x-ray vision on the dot, and sure enough it cut through the Dorkian glass. "Ha! Keep going," Melvin said. "Make a square."

It was the worst square this narrator has ever seen, but at least it had four sides. And it was big enough to crawl through.

"Let's scram," Candace said.

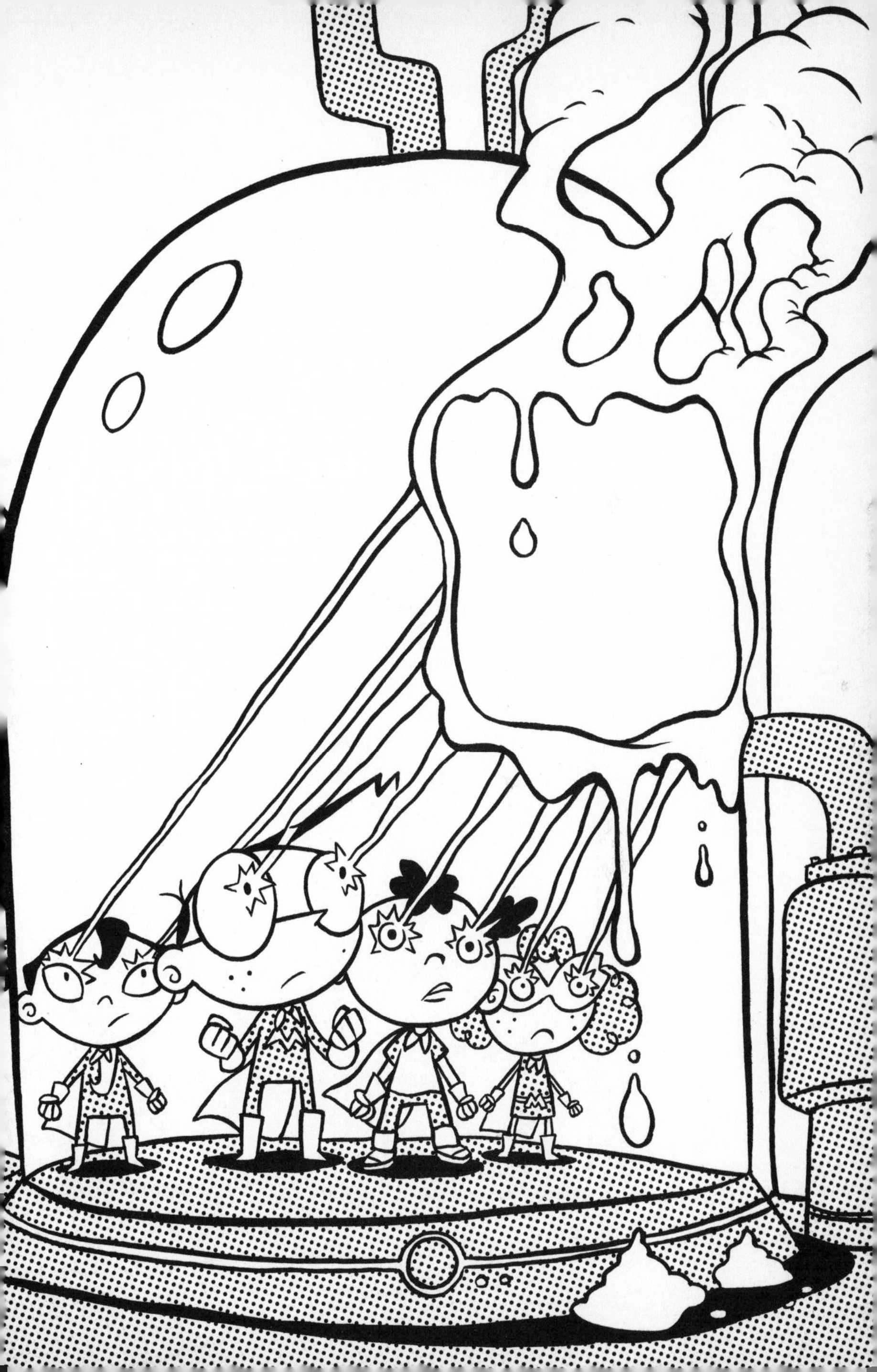

They did. They scrammed right through the new opening in the cage and headed for the door of the building.

"Ahem!"

Melvin and his companions stopped and turned. The caged alien was looking at them with that I'm-a-sorrowful-caged-alien look.

Melvin hesitated. What if he was one of *them*? What if he ate humans for a living? What if he smelled bad?

"I can fly that spaceship," the alien said. "I can get you back to your planet."

That was good enough for Melvin. He and his trio of superhero friends focused their x-ray power on the cage, forming another imperfect square. Once the alien was through, the five of them, plus Hugo, headed for the door.

"You got a name?" Melvin asked.

"Lester Vanderpeeb, but you can call me Ykrkvzz."

ALIEN DOG PILE

Once outside, they all ran for the spaceship. "Are you sure you know how to fly that thing?" Melvin asked Lester Vanderpeeb.

"Have I ever lied to you?"

Melvin didn't know how to answer that question. He'd only met Lester a few seconds ago. Still he seemed decent enough, for a guy with three eyeballs. Melvin wondered if he had more than one brain and if—

He stopped and sniffed. What was that nasty smell?

Stinky alien feet!

"They're coming back!" Candace yelled. "Look!"

"What kind of breakfast was that?" Melvin said.

Aliens from planet Dork were known for their speed eating. And now they were coming up fast, stun guns aimed and ready.

Melvin knew it was their last chance. If the aliens caught them this time, they'd never get away. "Split up, everybody. Scatter."

Melvin and James sprinted across the school yard. After all, they were as fast as a speeding bullet. Maybe faster. They leaped a fence and headed down Laser Beam Way, which ran into Beam-Me-Up Boulevard. It was lined with odd-shaped buildings.

"Where are we heading, Melvin?" James asked.

"Beats me. I'm making this up as I go along."

Actually, it was the narrator who was making it up . . . but let's get back to our story.

"We have to get out of sight," Melvin said. "We need a place to hide." They stopped and looked around. "What I wouldn't give for an abandoned warehouse right now."

"I'd settle for an abandoned anything," James added.

Fortunately, Beam-Me-Up Boulevard was pretty deserted. There was not an alien in sight. Maybe the whole area was abandoned. Melvin decided to check and see. He reached for the nearest door. It was locked, of course, but that didn't stop Melvin Beederman, the kid who kicked down doors in his spare time. Actually, Candace was the door kicker, but Melvin did it too every now and then to keep up his skills.

Melvin kicked in the door. "Follow me, James."

Sure enough, the place did seem abandoned. Or if not abandoned, at least no one was around at the moment. Melvin and James located a stairway and headed upstairs. They found themselves in some kind of alien office. Pictures of alien rock stars hung on the wall. An alien computer sat on an alien desk.

James went to a window and looked out. "I wonder where the girls are?"

Melvin wondered too. Hopefully Candace and Margaret had stayed together. If they—

"James, get away from that window," Melvin whispered. He pointed to the floor. "Someone's downstairs."

James sniffed. "I don't smell stinky feet."

They stood motionless, listening. Something was moving around down there, all right. Maybe it was an alien rat or mouse, or some other alien rodent.

They heard footsteps on the stairs. No, it wasn't a rat. It was a somebody. Melvin motioned James over to the doorway at the top of the stairs. "Get ready," Melvin whispered. "We'll jump whoever it is."

A few moments later something appeared at the top of the stairs. Melvin and James pounced, knocking it to the floor. "Get the gun," Melvin said.

There was no gun—and no stinky feet.

"I just love a good dog pile, don't you?" the creature said.

It was Lester Vanderpeeb.

"Where are the girls?" Melvin asked
him, standing up and helping the alien to
his feet.

Lester shook his head. He didn't know.

CRASH! SPLAT! THUD! KABONK!

While Melvin helped Lester Vanderpeeb to his feet, Candace and Margaret were hurrying down Pluto Place, which ran into Six Moon Highway. The area was deserted. They were either in an unpopulated part of the city, or the citizens of Dork liked to sleep in.

Candace knew they had to stay away from Monkey Wrench, Elbow, and Shoe— and their stun guns. If they got zapped again, it would be curtains.

They turned onto Six Moon Highway and launched themselves into the air. "Up, up, and away!"

Unlike Melvin, Margaret was up and flying on the first try.

"Wow, you're good," Candace said.

"Yes, I'm not Melvin Beederman."

"I noticed."

Candace and Margaret stopped for a moment, hovering and looking back. There was no sign of the aliens. Maybe they'd given them the slip. Still, they had to find a place to hide. The aliens could appear any second.

Candace pointed to a nearby tree. "Over there. Let's get out of sight."

They flew to the tree and hid on a high branch—just in time. Just in the nick of

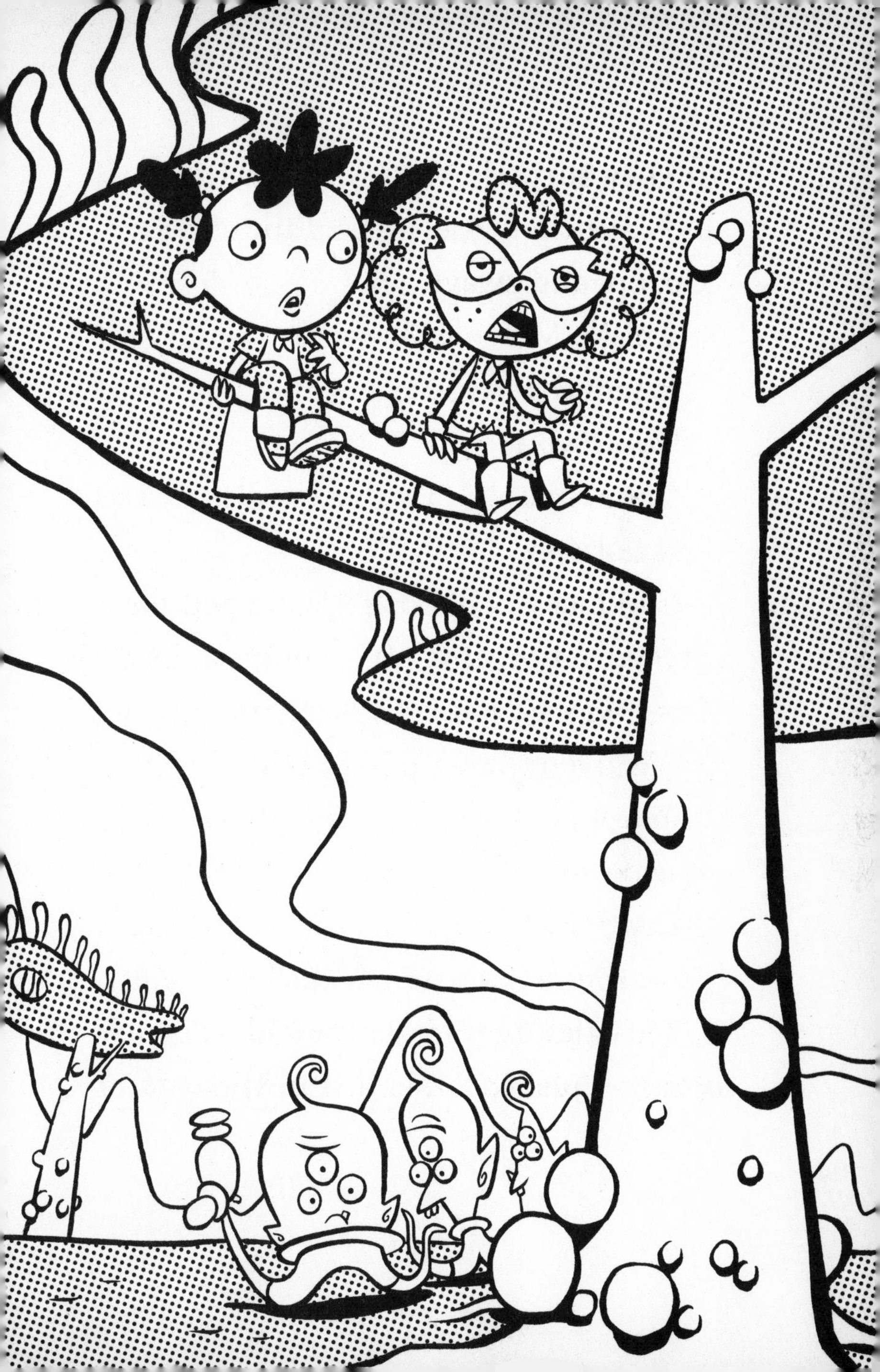

time, to be exact. Monkey Wrench, Elbow, and Shoe appeared around the corner on Six Moon Highway. They came closer . . . and closer.

Candace held a finger to her lips. *Don't move a muscle.*

They didn't . . . that is, until Margaret sneezed. *"Ah-choooo!"*

The aliens looked up.

"We're out of here!" Candace yelled. She and Margaret took off again, not bothering to say "Up, up, and away."

ZAP!

ZAP!

ZAP!

"Ha!" Candace said. "They missed us!"

She and Margaret zoomed ahead of Monkey Wrench, Elbow, and Shoe, being

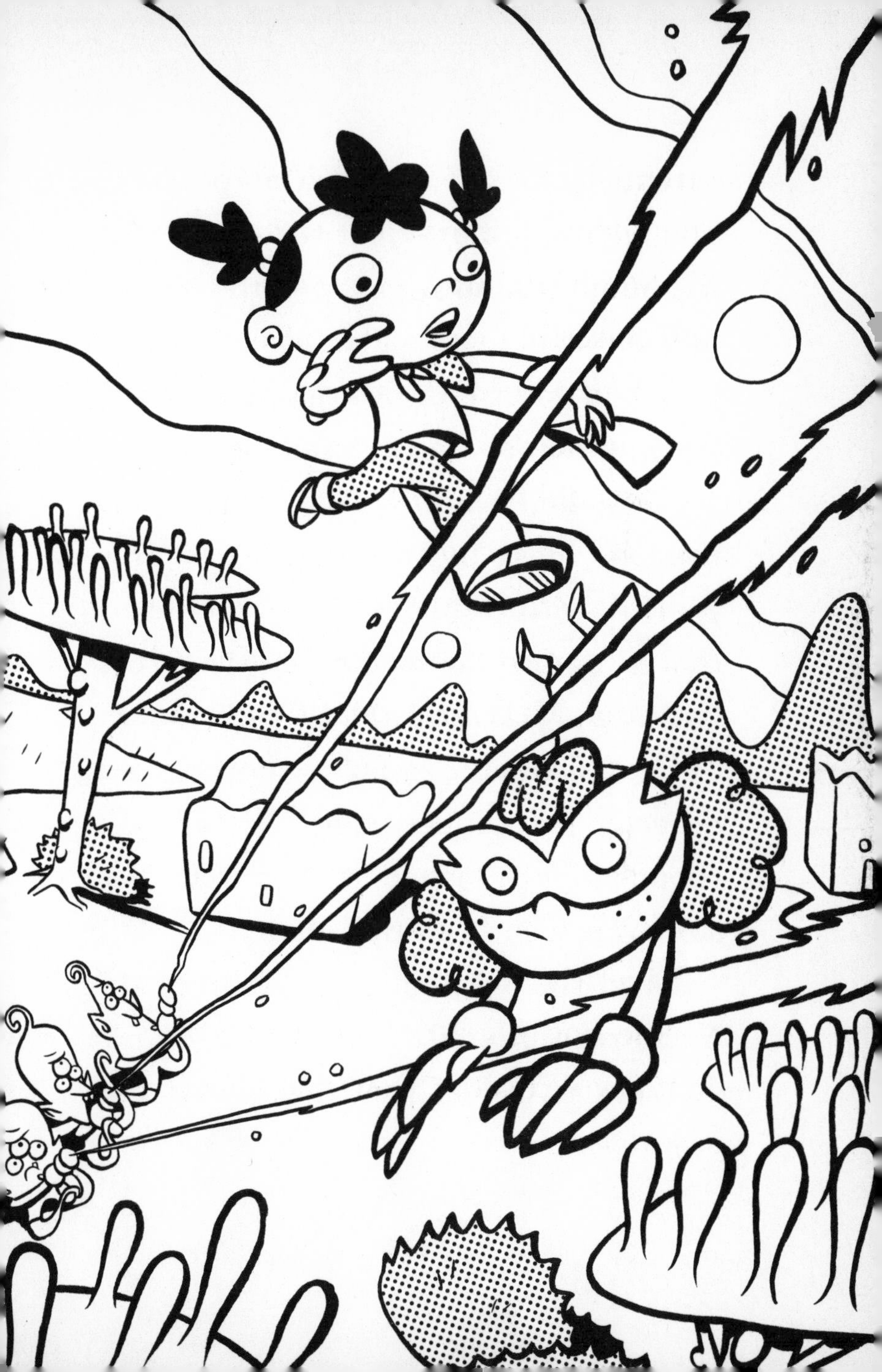

careful to zigzag as much as possible. They made a hard right turn around a tall building, and came upon the biggest mall either of them had ever seen. This is saying a lot, since Margaret was the superhero in charge of Saint Paul, home of the Mall of America. And not only was this one huge, but the parking lot was packed with vehicles—alien vehicles, that is. Banners hung on the sides of the building . . . *GIGANTIC ONE DAY SALE!*

"No wonder the rest of the city seemed deserted," Candace said. "Everyone's shopping." She looked at Margaret. "The stores open early on this planet."

"And me without my credit card," Margaret muttered.

"Let's go inside. They'll lose us in the crowd."

They'll lose the aliens by hiding in a crowd of aliens? It just might work.

But the bad guys . . . uh . . . aliens were hot on their trail.

"They're heading into the mall," Monkey Wrench said. "Split up. I'll take the front entrance. You two take the sides."

Elbow headed to the right; Shoe to the left. Things were not looking good for Candace and Margaret.

CANDACE MAKES HER MOVE

Candace and Margaret went inside, where there was some kind of food court—alien food of every sort. Margaret checked her pockets for cash. "Darn," she said. "I wouldn't mind getting one of those alien pretzels."

"Your money wouldn't work here," Candace told her. "We're on another planet, remember?"

"I guess you're right."

But it all smelled so good. They

walked passed Pretzel Palace, Galactic Gooburgers, Peter Planet's Pizza, Larry's Lunarfish Sandwiches.

Suddenly, Candace felt weak. She fell to her knees, gasping, "Can't . . . move . . . get . . . me . . . out . . . of . . . here."

"What's the matter with you?" Margaret asked.

"I don't know. I just feel like I can't—"

Just then an alien walked by holding a lunarfish sandwich. Candace felt even weaker.

"Their lunarfish must be close to Earth's bologna," Margaret said.

Candace nodded weakly.

Margaret picked her up and ran out of the food court. By this time, all the aliens were staring and pointing. One of them was coming their way. Margaret had seen him before—he was the one called Monkey Wrench.

Once they got away from the food court Candace began to feel better. "Put me down," she said. "I'm okay now."

Margaret did, but Monkey Wrench was still after them.

"Time to run as fast as a speeding bullet," Candace said.

And they did.

They ran as fast as speeding bullets. Maybe faster. They zoomed past Narnes and Boble Book Store, past May C. Jenney Department Store, and Worst Buy Electronics.

"Let's hide in there." Margaret pointed. It was an Abercrombie and Glitch. "Too bad we're being followed."

"I know," Candace said. "I could really use a new blouse or two. Even an alien one."

They ran through the store, looking for a place to hide. The dressing rooms were the obvious choice, but maybe too obvious. Monkey Wrench might find them.

"In there," Candace said, pointing to a clothes rack. It was the perfect spot for a couple of superheroes on an alien planet to hide while they figured out what to do next.

∧∧

While the girls were hiding in the clothes rack at the Abercrombie and Glitch, Melvin and James landed lightly outside the mall. James had been carrying Lester Vanderpeeb, who didn't know how to fly without a spaceship. Hugo sat on Melvin's shoulder.

"Thanks for the ride," Lester said to James.

They entered the mall food court. "Am I the only one dying for a pretzel?" Melvin asked.

James grabbed Melvin by the arm. "I'll buy you one after we find the girls," he said.

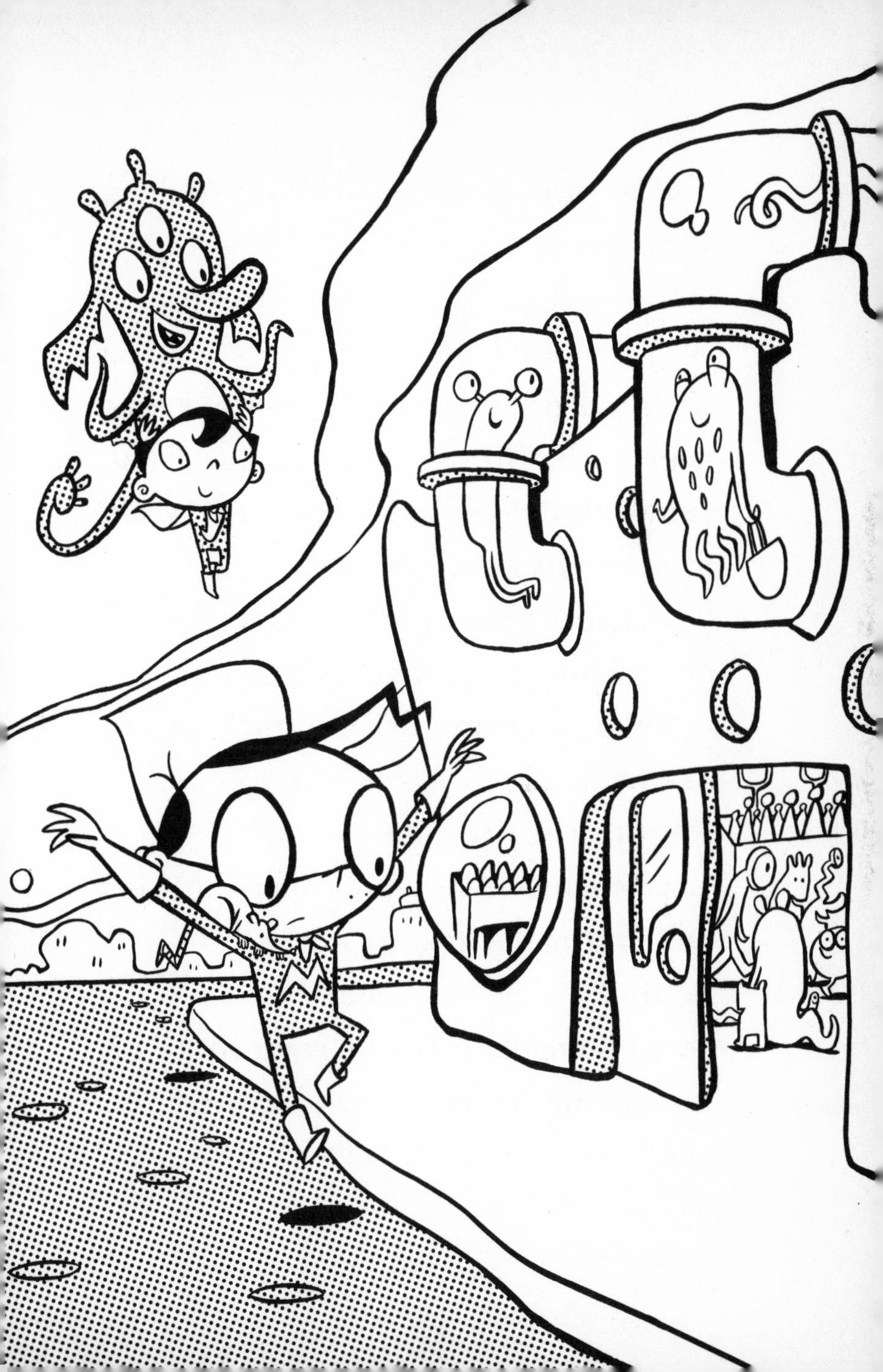

That sounded like a deal to Melvin. The problem was, where *were* the girls?

It was hard to think when everything smelled so good. They passed Pretzel Palace, Galactic Gooburgers, Peter Planet's Pizza, Larry's Lunarfish Sandwiches. Melvin suddenly felt weak. He fell to his knees gasping,

"Can't . . . move . . . get . . . me . . . out . . . of . . . here."

"What's wrong with him?" Lester asked.

"Not sure. It's almost like—"

An alien holding a lunarfish sandwich walked by. Melvin grew weaker.

"Must . . . be . . . something . . . in . . . the . . . lunarfish," Melvin said.

James picked him up and carried him out of the food court. Lester Vanderpeeb followed. So did Hugo. Once outside the food court, Melvin regained his strength and the trio ran . . . fast as a speeding—

ZAP!

ZAP!

ZAP!

ZAP!

But not fast enough. Elbow and Shoe's aim was perfect!

Elbow called Monkey Wrench on his alien cell phone. "We've got three of them . . . and the rat. Any luck on the other two?"

"Not yet," Monkey Wrench said.

While Elbow was busy talking to Monkey Wrench, Melvin noticed that his pretzel phone had fallen out of his pocket. He couldn't move his arms, so he dialed Candace with his nose. He had just enough movement left in his neck to do it.

"Shhh!" Margaret whispered to Candace. She peeked through the clothes on the circular rack and there was Monkey Wrench, a few feet away, talking on his alien cell phone.

RING! It was Candace's phone.

Monkey Wrench shoved aside the clothes. "Aha!" But before he could pull the trigger on his stun gun, Candace kicked it out of his hand. She caught it before it hit the ground.

ZAP!

This time it was Monkey Wrench who was paralyzed.

"How do you like that?" Candace asked.

"I don't," the alien said from the floor. "But at least I can move my eyelids."

"Now to find the boys," Candace said to Margaret.

It wasn't difficult to locate Melvin and James. They were the only non-aliens lying on the floor of the alien mall. Elbow and Shoe stood over them. They spotted Candace and Margaret coming—they were the only non-aliens running through the alien mall.

Elbow and Shoe pointed their guns, but this time Candace and Margaret were ready. Margaret picked up a trash can and held it in front of her. Candace uprooted a tree and blocked the stun guns that way.

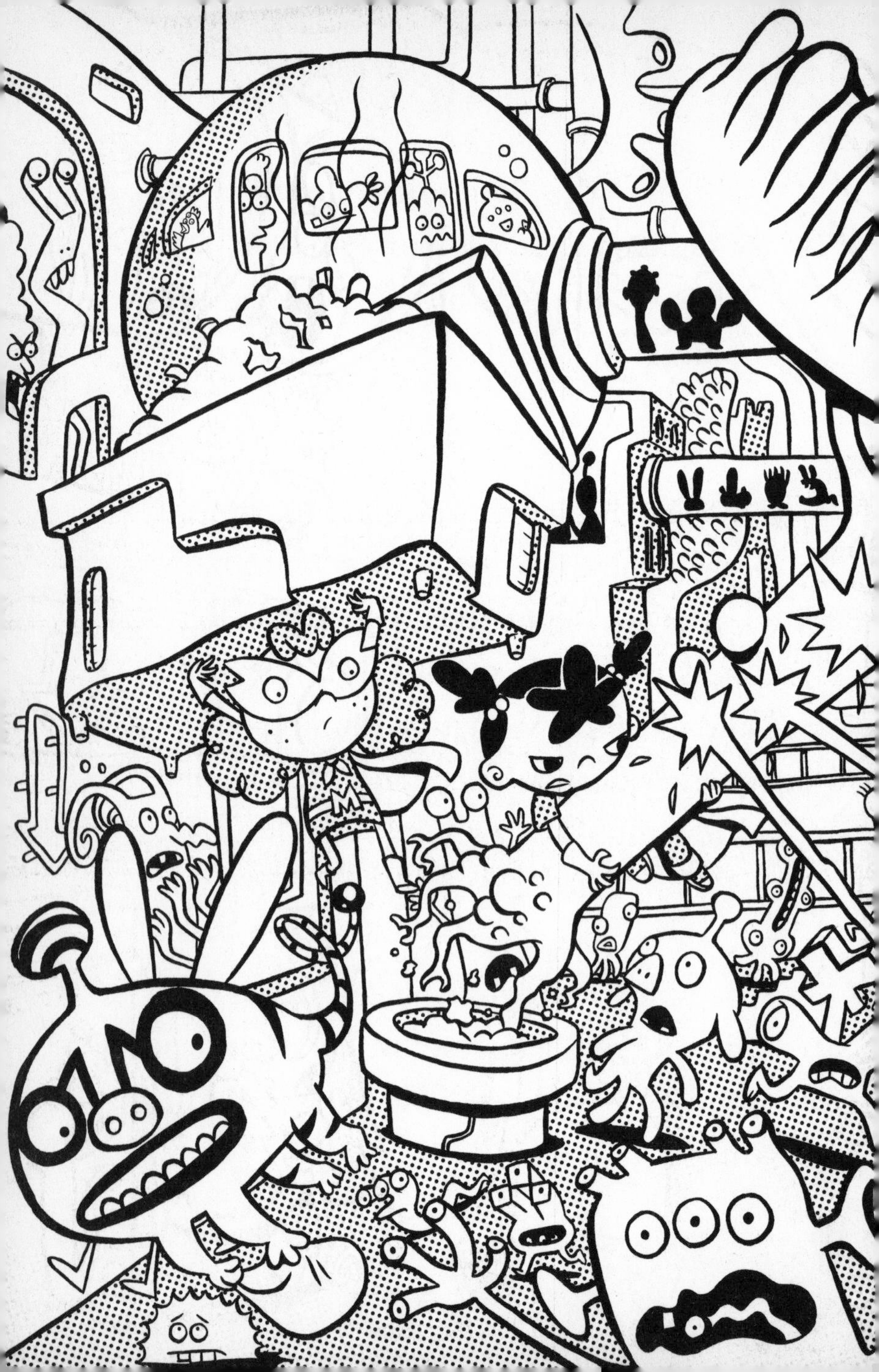

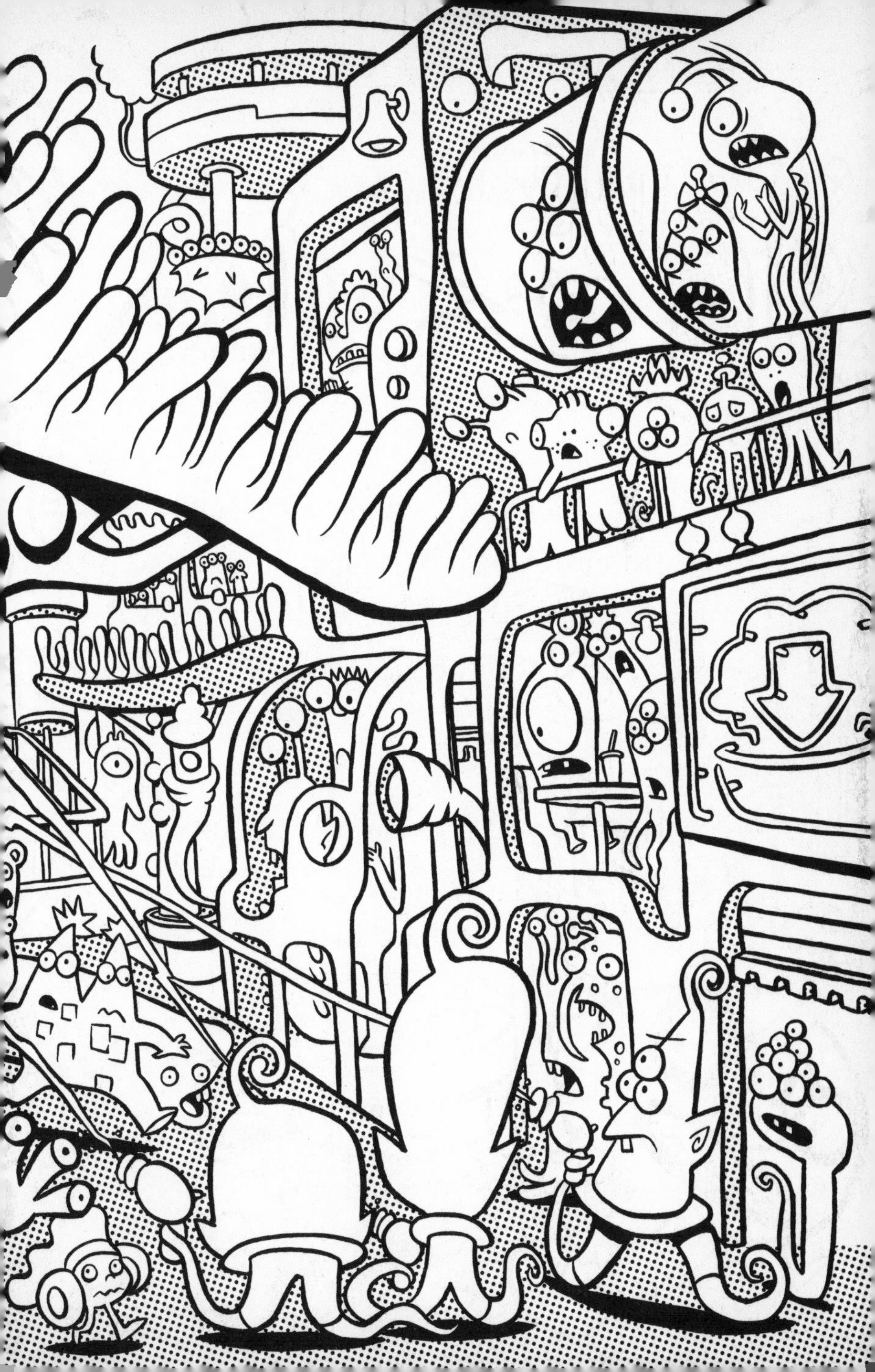

Candace and Margaret kept running.

ZAP!

ZAP!

Both aliens missed. Candace threw the tree at Shoe. Margaret scored a direct hit on Elbow with the trash can.

Both aliens fell, dropping their guns. By this time, Melvin and James were slowly regaining their ability to move. They picked up the guns and—

ZAP!

ZAP!

"How do you like that?" Melvin asked the paralyzed aliens.

"We don't." But at least they could move their eyelids.

"Let's get out of here," Melvin said. They all started for the exit.

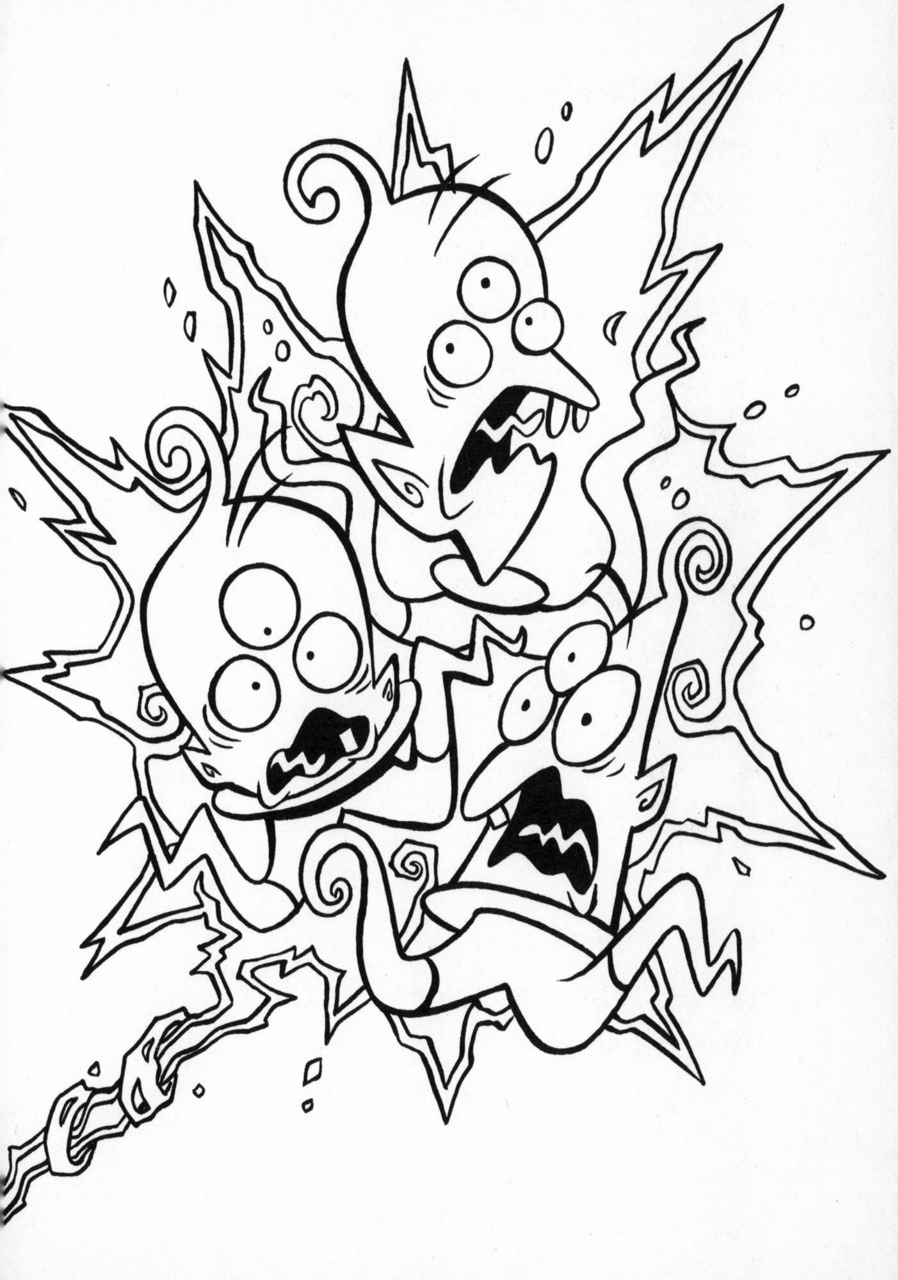

"Wait!" Candace said. "Not through the food court. Those lunarfish sand-wiches are bad news."

Too bad. James had promised to buy Melvin an alien pretzel.

THE JOURNEY HOME

Instead of going through the food court, our four superheroes, along with Lester Vanderpeeb and Hugo, found a side exit. "Up, up, and away!" Melvin shouted. Of course, everyone else was up and away on the first try. Hugo clung to Candace's cape. James held Lester. Melvin joined them on his fifth try, after crashing, splatting, thudding, and kabonking.

"It's a Melvin thing?" Lester said.

"Basically," James replied.

They all flew back to the school and climbed into the spaceship. "You sure you can fly this thing?" Melvin asked.

"Or my name isn't Vanderpeeb," their alien friend said. "Better strap in." Lester looked out the large window that spanned the flight deck. He saw Monkey Wrench, Elbow, and Shoe were coming up fast. "Time to scram."

They did. They scrammed—with a capital S.

James activated the cloaking device, which made them invisible. "Cloaking device activated."

James usually didn't use words like "activated." It just looks really good in a book.

Lester pushed a few buttons and pulled a few levers. They made the leap to Gamma Speed. A short time later they broke free of the planet Dork's atmosphere and sped through space, stopping only once—at Fast Freddy's Gas Station and Pretzel Barn.

"Holy alien-pretzels-are-great," said Melvin with his mouth full.

Holy alien-pretzels-are-great, indeed! It almost made the narrator hungry. Almost.

"I'll drop you off at Alpha Centauri," Lester said. "You can fly the rest of the way on your own."

"How are we going to breathe in outer space?" Margaret asked.

"THE SAME WAY SUPERMAN DOES!"

Melvin, James, and Candace said all together.

And so at Alpha Centauri, everyone said good-bye to their good friend Lester—he was pretty nice for a guy with three eyeballs—then they set off for Earth. Hugo sat on Melvin's shoulder for the trip. Just touching the cape was enough to allow him to breathe. You'll have to trust the narrator on this.

Soon they were breaking through Earth's atmosphere. That faster than a speeding bullet stuff comes in really handy sometimes. Everyone was in a hurry to get home. The sky was clear, but no one saw them coming.

Well, almost no one. At a nearby air force base, Private Gunther Whusterflap stared at his radar screen. "Sir, I am picking up four unidentified flying objects entering Earth's atmosphere."

"Four?" The commanding officer crossed the room and peered over Gunther's shoulder.

"Yes, sir. Should I patch you through to the president?"

"Not on your life. That's just Melvin Beederman and his friends returning from planet Dork."

"How do you know that? Have you been peeking at the manuscript again?" Private Whusterflap asked.

"Oops!"

Somewhere over Texas the four super-heroes went their separate ways. "Thanks for the help," Melvin called to James and Margaret.

"No problem," James said.

"Loved it," Margaret added.

They all did. They all loved it. It was what they did best—saving the world, defeating bad guys . . . and occasionally getting the best of an alien or two.

Melvin saw Candace home safely, then headed back to his tree house with his pet rat and partner-in-pretzel-eating. They were just in time for an episode of *The Adventures of Thunderman.*

"It's great to be home, Hugo," Melvin said, settling in on the couch.

"Squeak," Hugo replied, reaching for a pretzel. This either meant "You bet your sweet bippy," or "Dork is a great place to visit, but I wouldn't want to live there."

Melvin agreed. Even though planet Dork had great-smelling pretzels, Earth

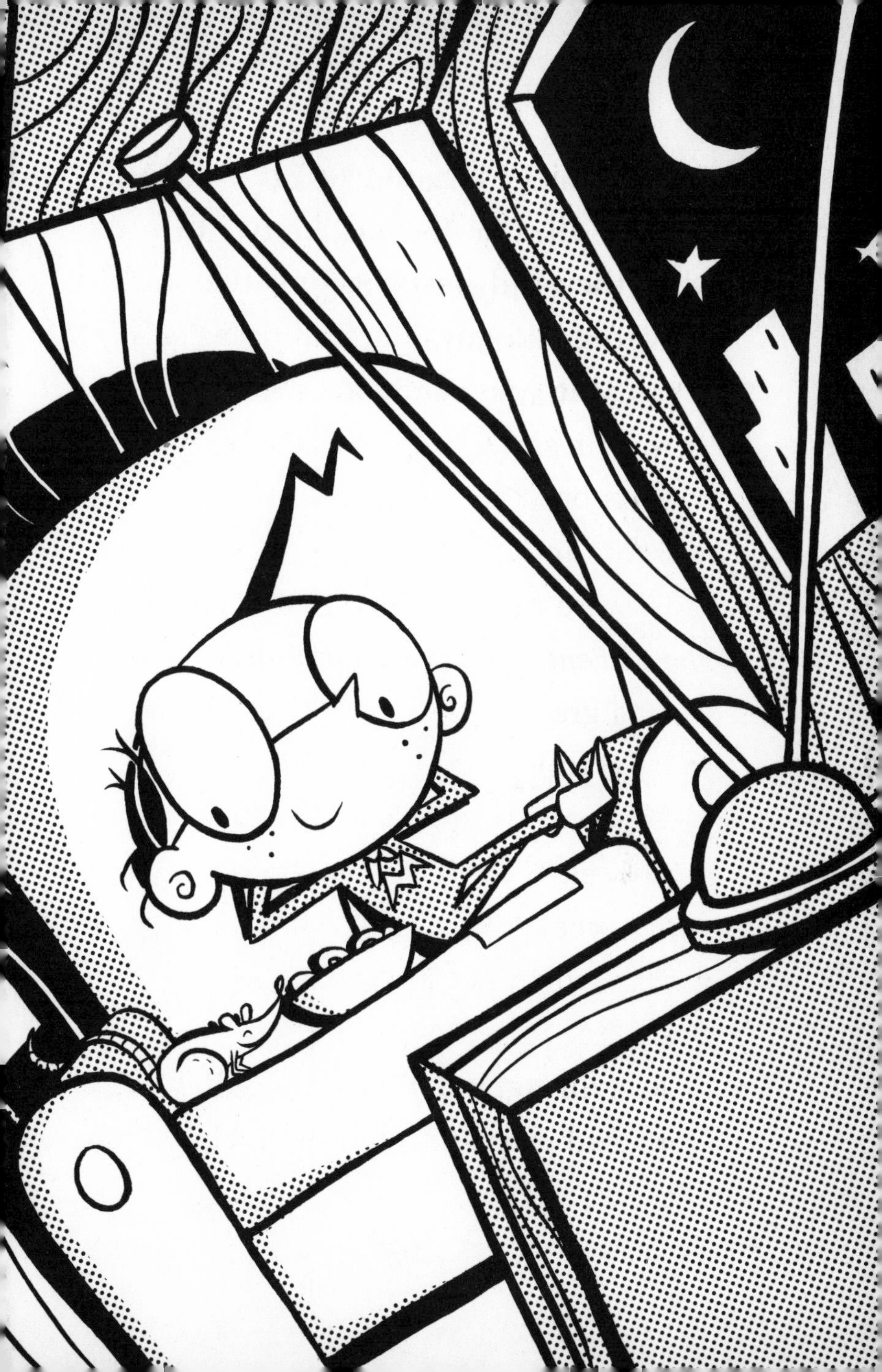

was where he wanted to be. He could hardly wait for his next adventure to begin, which was called—

He didn't know.

And that's the way the narrator liked it.